Book Four of The Deception Series

I0668280

Rape
by
Deception

Ryan Hodge

SMP PUBLISHING

This novel is a work of fiction. Names, places, characters, and events are either the result of the author's imagination or are used fictitiously. Any resemblance to actual people, living or deceased, places, businesses, locales or events is coincidental.

SMP Publishing Edition

Printed in the United States of America

10 9 8 7 6 5 4 3 2 1

ISBN: 978-0997799019 (PBK)

DEDICATION

Dear Ma,
Another year has passed without you here in the
physical form,
it's been thunderous without you, but you raised us
to survive any storm.
Sometimes different emotions come down swiftly
like a swarm,
because when you miss someone an array of feelings
experienced is the norm.
Even in your going home our bond is unbreakable,
your eternal love for your children is undeniable and
unmistakable.
You showered us with love which is more precious
than any material gift,
your positive personality and outlook were always
steadfast and never makeshift.
Ma, your heart was pure and full of sharing,
you taught us to be grateful for what we have and to
stay away from comparing.
We'll never cease loving and wishing you were here,
our love for you is everlasting and shall never
disappear.

CHAPTER 1

"Put your motherfucking faces on the floor. I will kill everybody in here if you don't comply with my orders. I don't have much to live for and I'm prepared to die. The question is, are you? If you make any sudden moves, I will be forced to blow your damn head off," said the witness.

"I know this is tough ma'am, but we need you to tell us what happened next. Take your time if you need to," stated the prosecutor.

"The next thing that happened was pure chaos and evil. The man wanted to show us that he was serious, so he picked a customer at random and put his gun in her mouth and made her beg for her life. Even after she did what he asked and begged for her life, the robber pulled the trigger of the gun and blew her head off," the witness testified.

"Ma'am, where were you when all of this happened? Also, do you see the person in the courtroom responsible for the robbery and murder?" inquired the prosecutor.

"I was sitting on the floor about five feet from where it happened and had a clear line of sight when he shot her. I saw her lifeless body fall to the floor and I was even covered in blood from the incident. I'll be scarred forever. The person who shot her is sitting at the table right there," answered the witness as she pointed toward the defendant's table.

The prosecutor uttered, "Let the record reflect that the witness has identified the defendant, Mark Wollinsky, as the robber and shooter."

Being in the courtroom for that case was my first time ever being in a courtroom. I was a junior in high school when I first discovered that I wanted to be an attorney. That day in the courtroom made me realize that being a lawyer was my calling and I set a goal to practice law from that moment on. I fell in love with the suspense, battle of the wits, and the chance to get guilty people off the streets. The courtroom is like survival of the fittest and it intrigued me.

I guess it makes sense that I always watched those old court shows like Perry Mason and Matlock. I even loved the detective shows like Columbo and Barnaby Jones. I have always had a penchant for the process and the finite details of a situation. I've always been a person to do ten times more research than what's really needed and that's a strength of mine. It's just who I am.

Here it is, many years later and my dream is about to be realized. Earlier today, I received my passing score on the bar exam. It's no big surprise that I passed on my first attempt because I graduated number one in my law class. This is one of the best feelings I've ever had. I feel a sense of euphoria and optimism. All of my family back home is proud of me. I'm the one who made it out. I come from humble beginnings. We weren't poor growing up, but we weren't rich either. We had just enough to make ends meet on most days and on occasion we had a little extra.

The city of Linden, where I grew up in New Jersey, has a mixture of residents. Some citizens of Linden are very well off, some are right in the middle, and some are starving to eat. I went to school with people from all socio-economic classes. I had gifted classes with the rich kids and had gym and played sports with the poor kids. It didn't matter to me how much money they had. I just liked to hang out with people who were cool and fun to be around.

I can say that I benefited tremendously from having friends with rich parents. They exposed me to many of the finer things in life. Their parents were also very influential in the business world. In fact, one of my friend's parents wrote a letter of recommendation that sealed the deal on me getting into the law school of my choice.

They were very helpful. My friends' parents who were poor were good people too. They motivated me to leave Linden and become somebody. They told me to always dream big and to never forget about them. I will never forget about them. They all played a pivotal part of my success. Whenever I have a free minute to go back to visit them, I do. I can't turn my back on them. I at least send a text to my extended family of friends and friends' parents to let them know that they are appreciated. They have always supported me. I do have to be careful how much interaction I have with some of my friends back home because not all of them have made the right choices in life. Some of the guys I went to high school with are real hardcore criminals. Not that I'm judging, but the government is real strict when it pertains to the company lawyers keep. I keep a comfortable distance from them, but they know it's for a good cause.

All of these thoughts race through my mind as I sit at this table. Me and several other people who I attended law school with are out celebrating passing the bar exam at In the Mix. It's one of the most popular lounges in D.C. Everybody frequents this place. The crowd is always friendly and the staff is too. Sage, who runs the place, has a section reserved for us and our tab is on the house.

Sage announces, "Your accomplishments

display a great deal of determination and mental fortitude. All drinks and meals are on the house."

We appreciate his gesture, but I'm no fool. It's a business move. Sage knows we'll be making big money at some point and will remember his kindness. He expects us to come back some day and spend boatloads of money in here. His kindness is an investment in himself. Either way, I'm enjoying myself now. We're all having a great time and the adult beverages are incessant. My friends all comment on what a good host Sage is.

"Alex, you've always been a good person and exceptional at what you do. I always knew you'd do great things. That's why I was so willing to host your event tonight," Sage voices sincerely.

"Sage, thanks. I appreciate it more than you'll ever know," I remark.

"No problem. I wanna make a toast to my main man Alex and to the rest of you," Sage voices for all to hear.

Our entire party is getting pretty wasted except for me. I'm drinking lightly because I'm the designated driver for Shannon. She passed the bar exam too. We've been pretty cool since the start of law school. Some of the bonds I've built with my classmates are unbreakable. We've pulled each other through many tough nights. For that, I'm eternally grateful to them. I remember one night when Shannon fell asleep studying, I saved her future career. We had a pact to call each other every thirty minutes and if the other person didn't call or answer, we would come over physically. That night she fell asleep and I went over to her place and woke her up. She ended up acing the test the next day. From that point, she felt she was always indebted to me. I'm an expert researcher and she's weak at it, so I always let her piggy back off me.

We have been at In the Mix for several hours and it's time to depart. Shannon has had way too many drinks tonight.

Shannon asserts, "Alex, I'm so glad you're driving because I'm a little tipsy and in no shape to drive home."

I respond, "It's cool. You know I don't drink much anyway. A couple of sips and I'm good to go."

"You helped my night be that much more enjoyable," Shannon states appreciatively.

"I'm glad I could help. Tonight is pretty special! This ranks right up there with the best of them," I say.

We say our last goodbyes, thanks, and congratulations to our friends then and we leave the lounge. Shannon's place isn't too far from the lounge, so we arrive in just a few minutes. She talks about places where she would love to work. As for me, I'm set already. When I was in college I interned at Mullins and Philbert, which is a longstanding and world renowned firm. They are worth well into the hundred millions of dollars. They decided to hire me after I passed the bar. I'm starting as their Corporate Attorney next month. Mullins and Philbert is an extremely demanding company and getting hired by them is no easy feat. Shannon and I even contemplate the idea of eventually opening up a firm together.

"The possibilities are endless," I boast.

"I know! It seems like we have just opened ourselves up to a whole new world. I'm super excited about what rests before us," says Shannon.

"We're truly blessed. There's no other way to state it. To see how proud my parents are is priceless," I state.

"Yes, and I know I have a bunch of loans, but I'm about to be making plenty of money. All I see is new handbags, shoes, and clothes!" Shannon details happily.

We both laugh as Shannon gets out of my car. As Shannon stands up, I notice she's a little wobbly and she falls back into the seat. I immediately get out of the car and head to the passenger's door to assist her. I help her stand back up and volunteer to walk her to her place.

"No, I'm okay. I just needed to get my bearings straight. I can walk," charges Shannon.

I state, "Okay, I won't take your word for it. Here's the deal. If you can walk five feet in my direction without stumbling, I'll let you walk all the way to your place."

"Five feet is nothing. I can walk five feet with my eyes closed," Shannon remarks.

Shannon takes four steps forward and five steps backwards. She stumbles back into the car seat, but not without injury. Unfortunately, her head doesn't miss the clearance of the door. She hits the back of her head on the inside frame. When I notice her stumbling from the blow to her head, I flash to her to try to keep her from falling, but I wasn't fast enough. Lucky for her, she didn't fall forward. She falls backwards into the car and lands on the front passenger's seat.

I ask in a concerned voice, "Are you alright?"

As she laughs, she states, "I'm fine. My pride is a little hurt, but I'm okay."

"I don't know about that. You smacked the back of your head pretty hard. Let me look at it," I say.

She sits up, so I can examine her head. There's a pretty large sized lump on the back of her head. I'm surprised that she's not unconscious. She isn't the biggest or toughest woman in the world, but she's taking the blow fairly well. Maybe the alcohol is making her a little numb.

"Is there a knot?" Shannon asks.

"Definitely. A big knot," I say.

"It looks like you have a big knot too," Shannon replies.

"What? I'm confused. What are you talking about?" I ask.

"Well, your crotch is point blank in my face while you're rubbing my head. I can't help but notice that you have a big knot in the front of your pants. Women always notice a man's crotch," Shannon explains.

"It does the job. I haven't had any complaints about him," I state.

Shannon replies, "I bet you haven't."

She then begins to rub my crotch from outside my pants. I don't know what to do. My manly senses want to whip it out and let her taste it, but I don't know if she's just acting and talking silly. She is a bit intoxicated. For every stroke I give her knot, she gives my knot a stroke too. She eventually takes my penis out of my pants and boxers and begins to lick and suck it. At this point, my mind is blown because this is totally unexpected and random. She stops for a moment.

Shannon states, "I had no idea your knot could get so swollen. This is nice! I can have a lot of fun with a cock like this!"

"I'm all for having fun! Let me take you upstairs and I can show you all of my fun tricks," I emphatically state.

Shannon shakes her head indicating 'no' and begins to taste my knot like she was previously doing. She's even more passionate and aggressive this time about her task at hand. I'm enjoying what she's doing to me, but there's a catch 22. I'm standing in a car door with my penis out in a parking space on a city street. I'm just not comfortable. For this reason, I stop her for a moment.

"If you really want to feel all of him, let's go upstairs and really get the party started," I say.

"I have a better idea. You can have me right here and now. In the moment…spontaneous. No prepping or planning," Shannon offers.

She climbs in the backseat and says her knot needs to be rubbed again. She will not move until I rub her head. I'm still erect and she begins massaging my penis with her hand. Before long, she's doing her same stunt she was doing in the front seat. I'm really enjoying her lip and tongue action.

"I want it! And I want it now!" Shannon screams.

I know I don't have any condoms and my conscience is talking to me. I could get her pregnant or catch an STD. She wants it badly and I don't want to disappoint her. I want it too, but not in the car. I decide to pick her up and take her into the house.

"I'm taking you in the house," I say.

I've always wanted to have sex with Shannon. The first time she walked into our first law class, I thought about having sex with her. I mean she's drop dead gorgeous with the perfect hour glass figure. Her natural blonde hair was cascading down her back as she seemed to float to her seat. Every guy in the room couldn't resist stopping what he was doing and watch her long tone legs strut across the classroom.

Her walk was one of confidence and strength without a hint of arrogance. At that moment, I pictured myself kissing her strawberry colored lips while being lost in her sapphire blue eyes. She has natural beauty with no blemishes on her face and doesn't wear much makeup. Now is my chance to attain one more thing that I've coveted for many years and I don't want to blow it.

My dick is still exposed and fully erect. As I reach into the backseat to pick her up, she tears off her panties, pulls me down, and jumps on top of me. She inserts me into her vagina and begins riding me in the backseat. I try to lift her, but my arms are pinned down underneath me. Eventually, I just give up and let her have her way with me. She's intent on getting what she wants and it shows. She's alternating between intensely riding my dick and sucking it, all while talking dirty. She's grabbing her nipples, squeezing her breasts, and smacking her own ass. She's even grabbing her neck and slightly choking herself. Then she begins to play with her nipples again; almost to the point I think she's going to rip them off. As she continues to ride my wild horse, she licks her finger and plays with her clitoris. I believe the alcohol has taken her to another freak level. The sex is amazing and I'm enjoying every moment of it. I take advantage of an opportunity to unpin my hands, so I can take a more active role. We're kissing all over each other's bodies. I'm caressing one breast as I kiss and suck the other.   Shannon is really enjoying this bit of ecstasy because she digs her nails into me as I penetrate deeper and deeper.   We're totally engulfed in the moment.

About five minutes later, it happens. I see a bright light flashing through the window. It's the damn police!   This isn't what I envisioned happening tonight. Fuck, I just passed the bar and this will decimate my career! Shannon jumps off of me immediately and tries to cover up with her clothing.

"Oh my God! Oh my God! We are soooo screwed! We'll be disbarred before we even have our first case," Shannon says.

"Calm down. I'll handle it," I vocalize.

"What are we going to do?" she asks.

"We will just play it cool. He'll understand. I'm sure he has done this before. He was young and having fun at some point in his life," I explain.

The cop taps the car window and instructs me to keep my hands where he can see them and to step out of the car.   I comply with his instructions. He asks me a series of questions about the current situation. I tell him that we were just fooling around a bit and it wasn't much more than that. The officer escorts me to the front of the car and instructs me to place my hands on the hood. Naturally, I comply.

He then goes to the car and asks Shannon if everything is alright. She's crying uncontrollably.

She can't gain her composure. She's scared, embarrassed, and slightly drunk. I just want this to hurry up and be over. He eventually commands Shannon to step out of the car.

By now, another unit has arrived. It really looks like there's a major crime being committed here. Multiple cop cars in the middle of the night are never a good sign. This is like the twilight zone. Shannon is now fielding questions.

"Ma'am, I notice that you seem a bit disturbed. Tell me what's going on," orders the officer.

While stuttering, Shannon states, "I… I have a terrible headache. This… this knot on my head."

"Did this man assault you?" he asks.

Another cop on the scene searches the car and finds a pair of torn women's underwear. He walks over to the officer interviewing Shannon to share what he has discovered.

The officer speaks, "The female also has a knot on her head and visible bruising around her neck."

Before I know what's going on, one cop has drawn his weapon on me and two others have grabbed me forcefully and thrown me to the hood of the car. Still rather confused about them grabbing me, I begin to resist their attempts to cuff me. They get more aggressive with every attempt I make to resist. They even take out their night sticks and hit me a few times to calm me down. The blows from the night sticks hurt, but not enough to make me stop resisting. I'm enraged and my adrenaline is pumping, so it's gonna take more than that to stop me.

They must have heard my thoughts because once they realize I'm not stopping my resistance they all stand clear of me. One cop takes out his stun gun and points it at me. He orders me to the ground, but again I do not listen.

"I'm not gonna tell you again. I'll give you three seconds to comply buddy," says the officer.

I don't drop to the ground in the time the police officer ordered me to, so as promised he shot me with his stun gun. As soon as the projectiles from the gun hit me, I freeze first and then begin to shake violently as I fall to the ground. Next, two cops dive on top of me and yank my arms behind my back and cuff me.

"Shannon, what did you tell them? What the hell did you tell them?" I ask frantically.

Everything is in slow motion. All I can see are the red and blue lights from the patrol cars speckling the dark of night. They pick me up by my feet and arms and throw me head first into the back of the police car. I sit up and look in Shannon's direction. I give her the vilest look of hatred ever given to another human being. As I sit in the back of the police car, I bang my head repeatedly on the patrol car window in utter disbelief. What the hell am I going to do?

Now, Shannon is being put into an ambulance and driven away. The cop gets in the car and tells me that I'm being booked for sexual assault. The cop begins to read me my rights and I begin to bang my head on the back of the passenger's seat. I gather myself.

"Officer, are you saying that Shannon is saying that I raped her?" I ask.

"Yes, that is what the young lady has told us. You are a loser dude. People like you make it hard for the good guys like me to get laid. I hope you fry for this," says the cop.

There's really no need to go into the particulars with this cop. He can't help me one bit. I need to speak with a lawyer. I know several of them, so that won't be a problem. I will tell them my story and this will soon be behind me.

The next morning, I meet with my mentor who's an attorney. He tells me that he was able to schedule a bond hearing for noon today. I'm elated because I will not be in jail for much longer. Knowing an attorney is a life saver in a situation such as this. He's doing all of this work for free. I would be up the creek without a paddle if it wasn't for him.

It's two p.m. and I'm finally released, but not after being photographed and fingerprinted. They took pictures of the scratches on my back. Shannon claims that they are scratches she gave me to defend herself. I wish I could just wake up from this nightmare, but this isn't one. This is the real McCoy. I hate Shannon right now. This is all her fault and now she's railroading me. Some friend she is. All of this for sex and I didn't even get to ejaculate.

My lawyer, James Bailey, tells me that my case does not look good at all. Shannon alleges that I brought her home from the celebration and asked to come upstairs. The report then states that I made sexual advances to her in the car. Eventually, I hit her in the back of the head and that's how she received the knot. Supposedly, I ripped her underwear off in an attempt to penetrate her vagina. She reported that she resisted a little, but was in a weak state from the alcohol and the blow to the back of the head.

I'm astonished. I can't believe that she turned the events of the night around to make it look like it was all me. She's afraid that she'll lose her license if she doesn't say I assaulted her, but I stand to lose much more. I have never been so angry in my life. If I go down for this, I'm never going to forgive her. All she had to do was tell the truth.

"James, do you think I can beat this case?" I ask.

"Alex, if you take this case to trial, you will lose miserably. There's too much evidence that is incriminating. Listen, no trial," says James.

"What are my options then?" I ask.

James responds, "I'm good friends with the prosecutor. Neither the prosecutor nor the victim want this thing play out for too long. They're willing to wrap the case up rather quickly, but you will have to do some jail time."

I scream, "Jail time!"

"Yes," James sternly replies.

"What type of time am I looking at?" I ask.

"You'll be sentenced to six months tops, agree to some probation, and community service. That will be the extent of it," reports James. "That is the best deal you are going to get. I think you should take it."

"What about the type of charge? Felony?" I ask.

"Yes, it will be a felony. There's no way to avoid it. And, unfortunately, you will have to register as a sex offender," James informs.

"Not the registry too? I will be finished. No one will hire me!" I scream. "I'm done and my life is over before it started," I utter in a devastated tone.

"Now, you can try your luck with trial, but I don't advise it. It's too risky. You could serve 20 years and your life will still be over. This way, it will be quiet and quick," James explains. "Look on the bright side; you'll do maybe two months in jail before they release you."

"I know. I know. Make the deal. This is a heartbreaking occurrence," I say as I put my head down and run my fingers through my hair.

James replies, "I will make the deal. I know this hurts, but let me know if I can help you."

CHAPTER 2

I'm a month into my prison sentence. I've never been to hell, but this has to be what it is. Fuck, maybe even worse. The food is disgusting to the point where I want to regurgitate just from thinking about eating it. I haven't seen a woman since I was brought to this facility, which is killing me. The worst part of it all is that I'm truly innocent. I never knew that innocent people were really sent to jail. Boy was I ignorant to reality. I can't even function normally because the threat of violence is imminent, inevitable, and ubiquitous.

The doors to the cells unlock with a loud clang. The sound they make reminds me of a big metal door to a dungeon being opened. That's a sound that I can do without. I'm sure it will haunt me for eternity. I exit my room and promptly head to the shower. I like to get in there as soon as I can because the showers aren't dirty yet. Also, many inmates don't leave their cells as soon as the doors open. I'm afforded an inkling of privacy this way. I'm at the tail end of my shower when I hear a sound more horrifying than the opening and closing of those cell doors.

"You the spineless bitch who likes to beat and rape women?" asks an inmate angrily.

"No, I don't know what you're talking about. I'm in for credit card fraud," I say to hopefully save my ass.

Another inmate who's accompanying him retorts, "Not only are you a rapist, you're a sorry fucking liar. He's the bitch who likes to take pussy."

"Yeah, I thought this was him. Well, since you like to rape people, we're gonna show you how it feels and give you a taste of your own medicine. You're gonna be our bitch today," says the inmate.

I decide not to be the victim. I hit one of the inmates in the face with a crushing blow to the nose. I nail him right on his nose with hopes of breaking it. Unfortunately, he barely flinches. It's almost as if I didn't hit him at all. The two men pummel me for what seems to be an hour. I eventually can't fight back anymore and become almost motionless.

"Now bitch. We whooped your ass like you did that defenseless woman, now we gonna take your ass like you did that defenseless woman.

You gonna need stiches in your ass after we finish with you!" screams one of them. "That could have been my sister you raped."

"You probably have been doing this your whole worthless life," replies the other inmate.

The inmate rips my towel from around my waist and I know that this is the scene I heard about countless times growing up. Everybody knows that inmates don't take very well to rapists and child molesters. I wish they could read my mind and see that I'm neither.

In my mind, I'm accepting that I'm going to be gang raped in this shower. I don't even know how they found out what I was convicted of. I try to squirm away, but my efforts are futile. One of the inmates pulls out his dick and is about to insert himself in me when I hear the most angelic sound I have ever heard. I hear the sound of correctional officers ordering the two inmates off of me. I'm saved from being violated. The correctional officers restrain the men and take them away. I'm taken to the hospital outside of the prison because my wounds are pretty severe. I'm just glad to be out of the prison. I spend the duration of my sentence recovering from my injuries.

Within a month, everything is settled. I'm out of jail, my career is shot, and I'm a registered sex offender like I'm a predator or something. I saw my life being somewhere else at this point, but I have to deal with what is now and before me. I know Shannon is interviewing for a job at Mullins and Philbert and will probably land it. She's living her dream life and I'm living in a hellhole. This is not even close to being fair.

I've been back home to visit my buddies who live there. Not all of them know what happened to me and I choose not to tell them. I don't want them to feel like they have no inspiration because I didn't make it big. I missed being able to hang with certain friends because of their checkered pasts anyway. Fortunately, they still love and support me.

I have plenty of free time these days, so I picked up a bartending shift at In the Mix. Sage gave me a job and gave me some pointers on how to be successful even though I'm down and out right now. He's always at the bar, so we've built a strong rapport. He's a bit arrogant at times, but he helps people when he's able to do so.

As luck would have it, Shannon comes into the lounge today and wants to talk. She received word through the grapevine that I'm employed here. She's lucky this isn't a dark alley because I would stick her right now if it was. When she approaches the bar, I walk to the supply room. I don't have anything pleasant to say to her, so I shouldn't deal with her. I'll most likely lose my temper and go off on her and may lose this job. This is a cool place to work and I need the money. Sage comes into the supply room to let me know Shannon wants to speak to me.

"I'm a little more upset than I thought I'd be. I'm not talking to her today," I say.

Sage replies, "You can't run from her forever. This is the first step to taking your life back. Be a man and conquer your anger."

"You're right. I'll do that. I have to move on," I reply.

Sage states, "Of course you do. I have her set up at booth three. It's quiet over there and you two can talk. Ask her why she treated you so poorly? Just get it out, so you can get past it. If you feel things are getting too heated and you need intervention, just throw up the sign. I'll be right at the bar."

"Cool, thanks man. I appreciate it," I say.

"Just get back on track," Sage orders.

I leave the supply room and head to booth three where Shannon is. I'm livid at what she did to me, but seeing her is refreshing. She's even more beautiful than she was before. I still remember how good it felt to be inside of her for those few minutes. I have to put my game face on though. I can't let her know I have a sensitive place in my heart for her right next to the anger. It's a mind boggling thing to love and hate someone all in the same moment.

"Hi, I was told you wanted to talk to me about something," I voice.

"Yes, I want to start off by saying I am truly sorry for the things that transpired on that night. It was a very chaotic night for me," says Shannon.

"For you!!! You?! My life is in ruins because you through me under the bus! I'll have to hit the lottery to bounce back from what you did to me. And you talk about for you? You gotta be fucking kidding me," I say angrily.

"I know you are angry and you should be. I would be too, but you don't have to live in such a cold dark place. You can win too," Shannon states.

"Hell, I physically live in a dark place. I live in a fucking hovel because of you! I can't move on until you tell me why. I just need to know for my sanity," I say as tears of anger stream down my face.

"When the cops came that night, I panicked. I saw my life going down the drain. I would've been embarrassed and my family would've been too, so I went along with it when the cop asked if you raped me. There was no sense in both of our lives being ruined. I knew the cops would believe me because of the bump I sustained to my head when I fell and the marks on my neck. I also knew my vagina would have your DNA because you weren't wearing protection and the ripped panties just sealed the deal. What I did was wrong. I admit that, but now I'm in a position to help you," Shannon narrates.

"You looked out for yourself. We could have beaten that charge if we would have stuck together," I say. "If we would have gotten charged at all."

"It was too much to leave to chance. I buckled under the pressure. I never meant to hurt you," replies Shannon.

"Yeah, buckled is an understatement. I was beaten and almost raped while in prison," I say.

"Alex, I'm sorry that you were beaten and almost violated. I care about you and I want to make this right. Could you forgive me?" Shannon asks.

"I can see how you were feeling. It was a crazy night. I can begin to forgive you. You did help lighten my punishment," I comment. "But how exactly can you help me now?" I ask.

"Through some of my contacts from school and from a big help of a prominent attorney here in D.C., I've been fast-tracked. I'm an attorney for Mullins and Philbert and I work for myself outside of that. It's a tremendous amount of work involved. Really too much for one person," Shannon explains.

"I see where you are headed, but I'm a convicted felon. I can't work for you. You know that. The government will crucify you if you get involved with me," I say.

Shannon explains, "You can work for me off the books. Only we will know. Here is what I propose. You are very detailed and are a research machine, so you can work for me in that respect. I will let you know what I need and you can get it and I will pay you for it."

"It's almost like you will be two people.

Getting double the work done in half the time. I think this could work out. My pay will be tax free of course," I reply.

"Yes, this can be mutually beneficial. I know your work is superlative and I really want to make things as right between us as possible," Shannon suggests.

"If your offer comes with some upfront money, I'll gladly work for you. I have to have some cash to pay bills with and eat until I get my first payment from you," I express.

Shannon hands me a bank envelope with money in it. Shannon doesn't stay much longer, but before she leaves, she informs me of the other particulars of our agreement. She tells me that she will have a prepaid phone for us to communicate with one another. I'm not to tell anyone of our work agreement. I'm fine with that because I will be paid handsomely. I'm going to be an overpaid research expert. I will have to put presentations together for her, but that's a piece of cake. I can do that in my sleep. If I'm lucky, I will come out of this in great shape. Everything just needs to go according to plan. I now have something to be excited about. Hope is a powerful thing! I'm definitely giving up this job, so I can work for Shannon.

"Sage, it's about to be on, but I have to stop working here. Something promising just came available and I can't pass it up," I state.

"That's great! You've outgrown this place

anyway and your aptitude says you belong elsewhere. I can tell. I'll love seeing you in a better position. That's why I told you to talk to her. As a matter of fact, I have a little parting gift for you. I'll go grab it," Sage replies.

"Okay, cool man. I appreciate gifts," I reply.

He hands me a small pouch. I can see a few things hanging out of the pouch. I see money, business cards, and some other items. He calls it a "get right" kit. I'm glad to have a few extra dollars in my pocket. Shannon gave me an upfront bonus, since today is my last day working here. This surplus of cash will definitely hold me over until I get my first payment from Shannon.

"Don't spend it all in one place. Use those contacts too; they may come in handy. That stuff in the pouch can get you where you wanna be," says Sage. "In fact, before you go, I want you to check out how to use the iPod touch I put in the bag. It'll be very quick."

I really don't need any help using anything electronic. I've been using Android and Apple products for forever. Since Sage has been a great employer, I go to his office and listen what he has to say about the electronic device. Thankfully, he didn't talk long and we're done.

"I'll use the stuff when the time is right. Thanks again," I say. "What you've done for me is priceless and I'll never forget it!"

Sage helps me out again. He has my best interest in mind for sure. I see why the lounge stays packed. People probably come more so to see him than to eat and drink. I wonder.

CHAPTER 3

The months have flown by since Shannon came to visit me at In the Mix. I have always heard that "time flies when you're having fun" and I believe it to be true. I've been having a blast these past few months. The deal that Shannon and I have going is better than I could have imagined. The money I'm making is ridiculous. My cash flow has increased exponentially in a short period of time.

This is even better than being a lawyer because I still have the freedoms of a normal person. I can get drunk and sleep in late without the fear of losing my job. The research I do is at my own leisure. I don't have to go to any corporate meetings or banquets. I'm able to travel at the drop of a dime as long as my parole officer doesn't find out. To make it even better, I can hang with my friends from all walks of life. I'm able to be myself - completely and fully. Most days I wake up and work in my pajamas. If not that, I go hang out at In the Mix and do some research or prepare documents for Shannon from there.

Every time I turn around, she has more work for me to do. I can only imagine what she's being paid if she can afford to pay me so handsomely. She must be getting well into six figures for her work. Because of my help, she's able to be in two places at one time, so I know she's sought after. Shannon has made it and she's a big shot. A well-known magazine even did a story on her about how she didn't let being sexually assaulted ruin her career. She's also the president of "Women Are Strong"- a national women's support group. More power to her because I don't need that limelight. I'd much rather things be the way they are now. I'm under the radar and making bank. Shannon even paid some of my student loans off for me. I think the guilt of what she did to me is eating her up inside. It works for me!

Shannon is knocking at the door now. She needs to pick up some documents that I prepared for her.

"How's it going, Shannon? I wasn't expecting you until 2:30," I express as I open the door.

"It's going very rapidly. Yeah, I know. I got out of a meeting early and figured I would shoot right over to pick up the things you have for me.

I hope I didn't catch you at an inconvenient time," Shannon responds.

"Oh no. Now is great! I'm just looking at some specifics of an investment company that I'm thinking about investing in. They're a small outfit, but I have researched the company and it looks like a potentially lucrative investment," I explain. "A friend of mine from back home started it up and says I can get on the team."

"Cool, in what type of things do they invest?" Shannon asks.

"According to what I have found over the last few weeks, they invest in stocks, real estate, bonds, and a myriad of other things. Check out their page," I say.

Shannon states as she peruses the page, "Wow, I'm impressed. It looks like they've invested in some profitable ventures. They even have some A-list people they have worked with."

"Yeah, they have. Everything I've researched about them says they operate very professionally. They're looking for an investor so they can take their company to the next level. I'm considering getting in," I say.

"I think you should go for it! It sounds like a great opportunity. I'm happy for you," Shannon replies.

"Great, I'm glad you think so. I really want to, but there's one hold-up! Unfortunately, I don't have the money, so I need your help to make it happen," I throw at her.

She asks, "How can I help?"

"You know my current employment with you pays me under the table, so I don't have a bank account. And even if I did, I wouldn't be able to justify how I have so much money without the IRS getting involved," I say.

"Ok, so what do you have in mind then?" Shannon asks.

I explain to her that instead of her paying me under the table like she's been doing, she can just write a check to Premier Investments and that will serve as my investment. She owes me money for work I've done for her, so this shouldn't be too much of a problem.

"I owe you a few thousand dollars for the work you've done lately. I can write the company a check for you. It is the least I can do for you since I'm the reason your work situation is what it is," Shannon verbalizes.

"Thanks a million! I really appreciate this. It means a lot. I thought I would have to miss out on a great opportunity," I narrate.

"How much do you plan to invest?" Shannon asks.

"They want fifty thousand dollars, but that is a little more than I'm comfortable investing. It's not like I'm a millionaire, so I'll invest what I currently have plus the few grand you owe me. I would extend myself if I had to, but I'm not really looking forward to being so exposed. However, investing the fifty grand would enable me to buy many shares of the company," I tell her.

"Yes, I know what you mean. That is a lot of money for you," Shannon retorts.

"Oh wow! You took a jab at me. You got me. Everybody's not as successful as you are Shannon. In fact, nobody I know is as successful as you are. You and I know fifty grand is nothing for you," I suggest.

"I don't know about it being nothing for me, but I have been pretty fortunate," Shannon says. "I wasn't intentionally poking fun at you."

"Okay, I was just checking. I thought you were trying to rag on me," I verbalize.

"Not at all Alex. You're my guy and I'd never do that. I made a huge mistake once that caused you a lot of harm and I won't do it again," Shannon explains.

"That's good to know. Shannon, I want you to know that I blamed you for what happened the night I was arrested, but after a lot of soul searching, I began to understand why you did it. That situation would have ended both of our careers. At least the way it went, you are in a position to help both of us," I orate sincerely.

"Alex, that means a lot. I'm glad you realize that it was a total panic move and not of malicious intent. Fortunately, it all worked out for the best because we're both in positions to make a lot of money," Shannon shares.

"Right! I can't let this opportunity slip through my fingers," I reply. "You gotta help me out!"

"Well, it does look pretty tempting. If you feel a little insecure about putting up the fifty grand yourself, maybe I could loan you the money to invest," Shannon utters.

"I didn't want to be too forward, but that's what I was gonna ask. Listen, I'll pay you back every dime of your money with interest. When I get paid, you get paid and that's a promise," I comment.

"You know what... I'm in! Your sales pitch is undeniable. I'm so sorry you aren't in the courtroom. You would've been great in there. I will front you the money and you just pay me back. No interest though," Shannon says.

"That's great! I will pay you back on time," I say.

"I know you will pay me back because I pay you. Just kidding," Shannon says with a smile.

"The investment company will soon be able to do all of their own work. They'll be or should I say, we'll be able to print what we need ourselves, hire more staff to distribute materials, wine and dine potential clients, and get more media outlets involved. We'll be able to house all of our services under one roof," I say.

Shannon cuts me a check, congratulates me one more time, and leaves to continue her busy day. I'll take the check to my buddy and he'll deposit it into the investment company's account, so we can get the ball rolling. I'll have to be a silent partner at Premier Investments because of my criminal record.

"Before you go, I have an off topic question for you," Shannon states.

"What's the question?" I ask.

"Who is the dashing guy in most of the photos you showed me?" Shannon inquires.

"Oh, he's Connor Bain. He's my buddy from back home, the founder of the company. Oh, so you think he's handsome, huh?" I ask.

"He definitely is an eye catcher. I'm sure he's taken. All of the handsome, motivated, and ambitious ones are," Shannon states as she leaves.

I leave soon after Shannon to run some errands. As I'm leaving the apartment building, I stop by my mailbox in the hallway to pick up my mail and I'm totally infuriated. There's a bag full of dog shit in my box. There's also a note on the bag that reads, *"This is what we think of you. You're a sack of shit. We hate sex offenders. Leave our community!"*

No matter what, no one will ever want to hear my story. Even though they may not want to hear my story, I'll be sure they do. I'm tired of these constant antagonizing behaviors. I didn't even do the things they think I did. I throw the bag on the ground and continue with my day.

I can't even give out candy on Halloween. The terms of my sex offender status state that I have to be indoors by a certain time and cannot give out candy. I have to look on the bright side,

I'm a free man making an honest living and for that I'm very grateful.

CHAPTER 4

My profits from Premier Investments have been very steady. In the six months since I made my initial investment, I have made about half of my money back. I expect things to really be profitable once I get my all of my investment back. The majority of the money I've made has gone straight back to Shannon. I wanted to try to get her money back as quickly as possible. I really don't like owing people money if I don't have to. She's being very professional about this too. When she receives a check from Premier, she immediately lets me know and asks me if I want to apply the check to what debt I have with her or if I need some cash for something else. In most cases, I don't need the money from Premier because she's still paying me for working for her.

Premier Investments is hosting a party at In the Mix this weekend. The event is expected to be one of the best of the year. In the Mix is always chosen as a venue anytime a major event is occurring. A lot of time and planning is going into making Saturday night a success and I'm excited. I'll definitely be attending.

I'm at Shannon's place about to give her some things that I've prepared for her and will be picking up some additional work.

"Do you want something to drink?" Shannon asks.

"No, I'm fine, thanks," I say. "Where do you want me to put these?" I ask.

"Sit them on the counter and pick up the other folder while you're over there," she replies.

I walk the files over to the counter as she directs.

"Do you think that you'll be able to have that back to me by the weekend?" Shannon asks.

"Have I ever missed a deadline?" I ask.

"No, you haven't, but there's a lot of work that goes into this assignment. I know you have a lot going on this week with Premier, so I figured I would ask," she explains.

"Well in that case, I'll make sure it's done. You have my word. Also, I want you to come to In the Mix on Saturday night. I want you to meet the man who started Premier Investments," I say.

"I'll have to see about that. I don't know what's gonna be going on by Saturday. I don't want to tell you I'm coming and not make it. You know how my schedule fluctuates.

Everything's fine one minute and the next it's all chaotic," Shannon says.

"Well, the way I figure it is that you need these documents back by the weekend. I'll have them done on Saturday and you have to pick them up, so you can come by the lounge for a minute to pick up the work and in the process meet Connor. You don't even have to stay long," I say. "Come on… he's a good friend of mine and you said yourself he's dashing."

"Ok, I guess you're right. I do have to meet you regardless and the lounge is closer to me than your place is. The time I'll save by not going to your place; I'll use to meet Connor," Shannon says.

I reply, "That's cool. This will be real informal. Two people on the path to success should meet. You may be able to help each other."

"Hey, I wouldn't be where I'm today if it wasn't for networking. You know the difference between a career flourishing or flopping in many cases is all about who you know," Shannon orates.

"That's right. The right people can really foster a career or the wrong people can just as quickly end a career. He's really a great guy," I say.

"Ok, great. Time for me to go. I have more than enough to do. I don't have it as easy as you do, Alex. Run, run, run is all I do," Shannon contends.

Shannon says that she'll definitely come to the lounge on Saturday. I inform Connor that Shannon will stop by for a few minutes. Connor seems excited to meet her. He has seen her in magazines and on TV and he knows that she could really help push the investment company. He also thinks Shannon is very attractive. I have to agree with him. I always wonder what we would have become if the cops hadn't shown up that night. I decide to start work on the assignment Shannon gave me. No sense in wasting time now and then be looking for the time later. I'll take the advice of Horace and 'carpe diem'. I will seize the day. That's my forte and always has been. I do what I need to do, when I need to do it. After looking at this work, I'm glad I started early. There's more research and intricate details than normal in this assignment. I'll be busy putting this stuff together all week. I guess it doesn't really matter because I don't have anything else to do.

This week has been filled with many hours of research, editing, and frustration. I also had a tremendous amount of errands to run for Premier. I'm glad the work week flew by because tonight is a big night and I could not wait any longer. I'm ready to kick back at the lounge and hopefully make a lot of money stemming from tonight's event.

I head to the lounge to help set up and make

sure things are in order. I'm fully invested in this company, so I don't mind some hands on work. Besides, Connor asked me to stop by to make sure things are going according to his instruction. As I drive up, I see many people walking in and out of the lounge with Premier Investments tee-shirts on. Sage agreed to have his people sporting tee-shirts with our company's tag on it. They're working feverishly. They look like people who are late for their flights in an airport. I park my car and go inside.

The place looks great! It's almost finished and looks like how Connor wants it to be. When they complete the finishing touches on it, it'll be perfect. It almost doesn't even look like In the Mix. The staff is doing a fantastic job. Sage and Sheena come walking out of the back as I look around.

"What's up?" asks Sage as we shake hands. "Just checking on things before the night gets underway. We want everything to be flawless tonight. No slip ups. I know you know where I'm coming from," I say.

Sage replies, "I sure do know where you're coming from. I'm making sure my staff is ready for tonight and making sure the shelves are stocked with plenty of adult beverages. The lounge could benefit from a great night just as your company can. This could be a very lucrative endeavor for both parties."

"I totally understand. Well, it seems like things

are in order here, so I'm going to split. I need to do some last minute running before showering and getting dressed for tonight. I'll catch up with you tonight," I say.

I leave the lounge to finish running my errands. I go home and get my clothes together for tonight. After that, I take an hour power nap, so I can be fresh for tonight.

My alarm clock is blaring an hour after I initially laid down. I wake up and clear my head. I get in the shower and get dressed. This is a super important event, so I want to be sure I'm sharp from head to toe. I spend a little extra time on my hair, grab my mints, spray on some cologne, and head out the door. I arrive at the lounge at 9 o'clock. The place is jam packed and it's still early. I can tell that tonight is going to be a great night!

I look for Sage as soon as I get there, but I can't find him. He's probably busy making sure his staff is aiming to please. I call Connor to see what time he's planning to arrive. I also call Shannon to see what time she plans on coming to the lounge. I really want those two to meet. They're both motivated and ambitious. Also if it wasn't for them both, I wouldn't be able to be a part of Premier Investments anyway. Both Shannon and Connor state that they will arrive at the party shortly.

All I see are dollar signs tonight. The line to get inside is wrapped around the building and we're charging twenty five dollars per person to enter the lounge. Additionally, there's already a large crowd inside the venue and they're visiting the bar frequently. This may be the best investment I ever made. The money we make tonight will help build up the company even more than my investment.

Around ten thirty, I receive a text from Connor letting me know he's inside the lounge. I text him back to meet me in Sage's office. I walk to Sage's office to meet Connor.

"What's up buddy?" I ask.

"Not much. It's looking good out there tonight. A lot of people came out, so all is well my friend," says Connor.

"I agree. It's looking like a handsome return tonight. We're getting twenty five dollars per person right now and in another hour or so we'll up the price to thirty dollars per person," I report.

"Not bad. Not bad at all. The place looks great. I couldn't have planned the decorations better myself," Connor says.

We both laugh because he is the one who actually planned the decorations to begin with. Connor has always possessed a great sense of humor. He's very witty and motivated. Connor consistently comes up with plans to make it big. He's one of the most enterprising people I know.

I say, "I told you this would be the perfect place to hold the party. In the Mix is happening dude!"

"Yeah, yeah bro. I gotta admit, you were right," states Connor.

"Hey man. You know I'm always right," I reply. "You know my word is golden."

"Well, I hope your word is golden about that other thing you told me," Connor verbalizes.

"Oh, you're talking about Shannon. My word is my bond on that. She's beautiful and intelligent. A real go getter. You'll love her man. You know, real down to earth even though she's successful," I narrate.

Connor replies, "Bud, she was pretty in the picture you showed me, but you know how photo filters can be."

As we exit the office, Shannon is walking in the front door. She's exquisitely dressed in a tight black dress and six inch stilettoes. Her legs are long and curved, cheeks rosy, and ass is the perfect plumpness. She definitely came to impress tonight.

Connor spots her before I get to introduce him to her. He's thoroughly impressed by her beauty and the confidence she exudes with each step she takes.

"She's even more beautiful than the picture you showed me," states Connor.

"I know man. I told you I wasn't kidding," I reply.

Shannon and I make eye contact and she struts over to us. We all go back to Sage's office. I introduce Shannon and Connor to one another.

Shannon compliments Connor on the way the lounge looks and they converse back and forth.

"Alex showed me a picture of you, but I must say it pales in comparison to your beauty in person. Thank you for allowing me the privilege to meet you," says Connor.

Shannon replies, "The pleasure is all mine. Thank you for such a thoughtful compliment. You're not too shabby yourself."

"I guess I will take that as a compliment," Connor comments.

"Yes, you should. It was meant to be," voices Shannon.

"I'm surprised you aren't accompanied by your significant other. Surely you have one," Connor says.

"Actually, I'm single. No extra baggage tying me down," Shannon remarks coyly.

"Well, this night is getting better by the moment. I would love to get you a drink," Connor speaks.

"That's funny because I would love for you to get me a drink," Shannon retorts.

Shannon and Connor walk off together to get a drink. Shannon and Connor really hit it off. They spend the rest of the night talking, laughing, and dancing. It's almost like they're the only two in here tonight. You would think they've known each other for many years. I guess the night is successful on two fronts. The party is a total success and Connor and Shannon made a union tonight. Connor even calls me over to take pictures of the two of them. After I take the pictures, he immediately uploads them to Instagram.

Shannon stays a lot later than she originally anticipated. She departs just after midnight. She and Connor exchange numbers and plan to see each other in the future. Sage finally links up with us for a few minutes. He jokes with Connor and tells him that he's been struck by cupid's arrow tonight.

"No, no, I know what it looks like, but it's only business. Nothing personal. She's a great business contact. That's all," says Connor.

"Right, that looked more like Romeo and Juliet. Shakespeare couldn't have written that better himself. You two remind me of when Romeo and Juliet met at the Capulet house," says Sage.

"That's funny. She's beautiful and cool, but it's only business. I assure you. Well fellas, I guess since we're talking Shakespeare dramas, it's time I exit stage left," shoots Connor.

We all laugh as Connor leaves. I stay until the lounge closes. I collect all of the money we made for hosting the party and then I head home. I will go to the bank on Monday to make a deposit into the company's account.

The party was a great success. There wasn't drama and everyone seemed to really enjoy themselves. I drive home immediately following the party. I'm surprisingly wide awake. I really expected to be drained after all of the partying and ripping and running. When I arrive on my block there are no available parking spots, so I drive to the next block and find a place to park. As I walk to my apartment, I see a silhouette approaching me.

"Do you have a light?" the stranger asks.

"Sorry, buddy. I don't smoke," I reply as I keep walking.

He replies, "I guess you're smart for not smoking. These things will kill you."

This guy is following me down the street trying to hold a conversation in the middle of the night. I don't know who this guy is, but I'm keeping my distance from him. I wish I had a gun or a bludgeon of some sort. Maybe I should just start running. There's no way he can catch me if I start sprinting, but where will I run to? I don't even know if this guy means me any harm. I'm probably just imagining things in my head. Those couple of drinks I had tonight are making me paranoid. I need to relax.

I hear the stranger say, "Hey man, you look familiar."

I don't want to make him angry and turn nothing into something, so I respond to him.

"Yeah, I get that a lot. Guess I just have one of those faces... heard it a thousand times," I state.

He responds, "You sure do! It's more like

infamous. I've seen your barbaric face before. You're that damn child rapist. I've seen your face on that sex offender registry."

As soon as he says that, I take off running. I know he doesn't mean me any good at this point. My initial suspicions about this guy weren't fraudulent at all, but were actually right on point. The guy starts chasing behind me. I can't run to my house because he'll follow me there and I don't want him to know where I live. I have to ditch this guy. I run right past my doorstep as if I've never seen that place before in my life. I decide to sprint to the next block and make several turns and cut through a backyard or two. This will lose him for sure. I know these dress shoes will slow me down a little bit, but I'm quick enough and have enough stamina to escape.

I stick to my plan and I lose this pretend vigilante. He doesn't even know the real story. What a fool! He called me a child rapist and my charge isn't even for raping a child. I wish I could have told him that I'm really innocent, but I didn't need to explain myself to him. He probably wouldn't have believed me anyway. Nobody would believe me because all criminals claim they're innocent.

My brand new shoes are pretty shabby from all of this running and fence jumping. Oh well, I'm just glad I got away from him. Who knows if he had ill intentions or not? I hope to never see him again. I enter the hallway of the building where I live and walk up the steps toward my apartment door when I hear the same voice asking for a light.

He says, "Next time don't leave your registration card in your car. You dumb bastard! Keep your hands off of defenseless women and children!"

He hits me over the head with a pipe and I fall against the door unconscious. I wake up sometime later in my bedroom with one of my neighbors sitting next to the bed.

I ask, "How long have I been out?"

My neighbor responds, "About three hours since I found you. I didn't know if you'd ever wake up. That bump on your head is pretty nasty."

"Yeah, my head is killing me. Some random guy attacked me," I say.

"Oh yeah, there's one other thing," she utters.

"What's that?" I ask.

"The person who attacked you wrote the word rapist on your back in red paint. I attempted to remove it, but was unsuccessful. I'm sorry," she speaks. "I think the person may have wanted to kill you. I don't want to scare you, but when I opened my apartment door the guy was standing over you about to pummel you with the pipe again. When he saw me, he ran away, but I didn't see his face."

"No. Don't be apologetic. You have been a great help. I really appreciate everything you've done. You potentially saved my life. That guy had the situation completely misconstrued. I'll resolve it though," I state.

My neighbor excuses herself and goes back to her apartment. I know I can't live here anymore because it's clearly too dangerous. That maniac who attacked me could come back to hurt me again whenever he wants. I can't live in constant fear of something happening to me.

Later in the day, Shannon stops by to bring me some things to work on over the next few days. I'm in bed when she comes in.

"What the hell happened to you?" Shannon asks immediately.

"It's a long story, but it ended with me getting attacked on the doorstep and my neighbor finding me. When I woke up, I was here," I narrate. "Fortunately, my neighbor interrupted my attack before things got worse."

"You could have been killed. Oh my God! Are you okay?" Shannon asks.

"I've been better, but I I'll be fine. It's just a knot on my head. Nothing too serious," I report.

Shannon asks, "Did you have a fight? Were you robbed?"

Instead of telling her exactly what happened, I sit up in the bed and lean forward.

"Look at my back. You know they say a picture is worth a thousand words. Well, in this case, one word is worth a beat down," I say.

Shannon looks at my back and bursts into

tears. She feels the guilt of falsely accusing me of rape. The fact that I was almost killed because of it makes her feel worse than she already did.

"This is all because of me, huh?" asks Shannon.

"We don't know that for sure. He could've mistaken me for someone else. You never know. Mistakes happen all of the time," I say.

"That's so nice of you to say to make me feel better, but it's not working. I feel horrible. Just horrible," Shannon replies.

"I don't want you to beat yourself up over this. I already took a beat down for the both of us," I reply jokingly.

Shannon says, "That is soooo not funny. You are making light of a very serious situation. You could have been hurt far worse than you are now."

"The great thing is that I'm not, but I do need to get out of here. I'm vulnerable here. That guy could come back at any time and cause more harm than he did today," I narrate.

"Yes, I totally agree. I would be frightened out of my mind coming here after what happened to you," Shannon says.

"I need your help to make it happen," I say.

"Anything you need. I'm glad to help," Shannon articulates.

"I need you to rent me another place. I'm obviously not safe here. If I rent a place on my own, my address will show up in the sex offender database. If you get it for me, I'll be able to come and go as I please without fear of danger," I dictate.

Shannon replies, "I understand your position. I know a place that's currently leasing and has very affordable rent. Bel-Aire Houses will be perfect for you and everyone minds their business. If you want, I can stop by there and fill out a leasing agreement for you."

I tell Shannon that'll be perfect and how much I appreciate her doing that for me. She lets me know that it's the least she could do and it's not a problem. She leaves the apartment to get things rolling with the application. I inform her that I don't expect her to pay my rent for me. We agree that she will just pay the rent out of the money she pays me for working for her. I'm ecstatic she's willing to help me. Knowing that I'm going to be out of here soon will help me sleep a little bit better.

CHAPTER 5

It's been three months since I was attacked at my old apartment and I really don't miss that place. I'm to the point where I don't think about the attack. It's funny how getting attacked enabled me to move into this fabulous space. Unfortunate situations sometimes turn out to be fortuitous. Talk about the forces of irony. I wish I could completely wash my hands of my former place of residence, but I can't. I still have to pay rent and pretend like I live there because of my parole situation. If I let the parole officer know that I moved, he will have to change my address in his system. That would force me to be identified in the sex offender registry in this neighborhood. I definitely don't want that. I loathe even going to get my mail from that hellhole, but I need to keep the front going. Every now and then, I receive some demeaning notes in my mailbox or disgusting looks from some of the neighbors.

I have to admit, Shannon has me living in splendor. I have many amenities that I did not have before. There's a washer and dryer in my new place. They even have a swimming pool in the neighborhood for residents and there's even a workout facility. My old apartment complex has none of these comforts. The only negative out of this situation is that I am paying two separate rents. I guess it's only money and plenty of that is rolling in. Thankfully, I'm financially secure right now. Working for Shannon and being an investor in Premier Investments are both keeping me busy, but they are also keeping me paid.

Connor and Shannon have become quite the couple over the last few months. They've been hot and heavy ever since they met at the party at In the Mix. They're almost inseparable these days. I knew it was more to it than what Connor let on when they first met. I've known Connor a long time and I can tell when he truly wants someone and he definitely wants her. There is no doubt about it.

I must admit they look great together. They're always taking pictures together and posting them on Instagram and Facebook. The pictures they post always receive numerous likes. They remind me of Angelia Jolie and Brad Pitt because they are so photogenic. Their presence is always felt when they're in the room. Shannon and Connor command attention no matter where they are. The two of them went to the Poconos for a weekend getaway a couple of weeks ago. Through some of Shannon's business contacts they were able to get skybox seats to a Steelers' game. I joke with them all the time about me hearing wedding bells. Shannon thinks it will happen someday, but is not sure when.

The sound of my phone ringing breaks the silence in my place. The only call that I'm expecting is from Shannon. Shannon said she's going to stop by after she goes out with Connor, so it's too early for her to be heading this way already. That was only an hour ago that she said that. They couldn't have finished their outing already. I look at the phone's screen and to my surprise it is Shannon. I answer the phone.

"Hey Shannon. What's up?" I ask.

She doesn't even answer my question and just begins shouting into the telephone. I can't make out what she's saying.

"Shannon, Shannon. Calm down. I can't understand a word you're saying," I say.

"I'm so fucking angry right now. I have never been so humiliated in my life. Fuck!" screams Shannon.

I ask, "Why? What the hell happened?"

"Connor and I are heading to your place now. I'll tell you the story when we arrive. We'll be there in about ten minutes," says Shannon.

The next ten minutes seem like ten hours. I

can't imagine what would have happened that would cause Shannon to become so upset. She's normally in good spirits. I'm throwing a myriad of scenarios together in my head before they arrive. Did they get mugged? No they didn't get robbed because that wouldn't cause Shannon to be humiliated.

Maybe they ran into one of Connor's ex-girlfriends and things got a little sticky. I have no idea. It could be anything. My mind is racing a mile a minute. I keep looking out the window for them to pull up. Finally, I see them turn the corner and drive up to the house. They get out of the car and walk to the door.

Connor uses his key to let them in, but Shannon comes through the door first and has a very troubled look on her face. Her demeanor is totally opposite from her normal. I hope Connor didn't put his hands on her. That's totally not his style. She doesn't say a word when she comes through the door. She looks like she's trying to calm herself down. Connor walks through the door, but he looks normal. He doesn't appear to be shaken at all. I'm completely confused now. I can't figure out how Connor looks as if nothing has happened, but Shannon clearly does.

"Hey bud. What's up?" Connor greets.

"You tell me. I'm scared shitless. Tell me what's going on," I say.

"My nerves are a wreck is what's going on. I need a drink," states Shannon.

I fix Shannon a glass of wine to help calm her nerves. She sips the drink and paces back and forth.

"Ok dude, spill the beans. Talk to me," I demand.

He states, "We were sitting in Close Fellows Sports Bar and Grill having a couple of drinks when I noticed some random guy looking at us from across the bar."

"You got into a fight over Shannon, didn't you?" I ask.

Shannon breaks her silence and states, "I wish that was it. At least that would make sense."

"So what happened?" I ask.

"If you would let me tell the story and not interrupt, you would have heard it by now," cracks Connor.

His joke causes us to laugh. It definitely lightens the mood which is clearly needed right now. Connor restarts his narration.

"I assume the guy is sweet on Shannon. That's no big deal. I know she's beautiful, so I expect that. Guys hit on her all the time when we go out. I'm secure in my position," says Connor.

"You're so cocky," states Shannon.

"It's not cockiness, it's confidence," retorts Connor. "There's a difference."

"The story please," I say.

Connor states, "The guy who was looking at me continued to stare at me constantly. Business is great, so I decided to buy the entire bar a round of drinks on me. Everything was going smoothly until the same guy approached Shannon and I. He began to tell me that I'm not the only one with money and that he doesn't need me to buy him a drink. He made a huge scene in the bar. After that, he started yelling that he doesn't like my kind and that I'm beneath him. The guy was clearly out of his mind and had me mistaken for someone else because I didn't know him from Adam. I took Shannon by the hand to escort her out of the bar, when the guy threw the drink I purchased for him into my face and it splashed onto Shannon too."

"I know you lost it at that point," I say.

Connor says, "The guy was about to say something else when I punched him in the jaw. Then I went to grab him to break his neck when the security workers stepped between us and sent all of us out of the bar. They even called the cops to the scene to talk to us, but it wasn't that serious to me, so we left."

"It was a fiasco. The guy was totally out of line and he should be punished like the criminal he is. I want to file assault charges against that asshole. He was totally out of line, but Connor wants me to drop it. I was livid when that drink hit my face," explains Shannon.

"That's so crazy! The guy was clearly upset because Connor's young and has money. He didn't want to be upstaged by you. I guess it could have happened to anyone. Or maybe he was jealous of you because you have a pretty woman on your arm and you have money," I say.

"Who knows what that shit was about. I'm glad it's over now. Things almost got way out of hand," says Shannon. "I can't be involved in any affrays; I'm a lawyer for goodness sake."

Connor comments, "Let's be for real, I don't think any of us can afford or want a criminal case. We're above that."

We chat some more and then my phone begins to ring. Now, who's calling me? Hopefully, it isn't any more nonsense. Shannon and Connor's news is enough for today. I pull my phone out a see that someone is calling from a restricted number. Foolishly, I answer the call.

"Hello," I say.

"You filthy piece of shit! You got lucky that I didn't get to finish bashing your fucking head in that night on your doorstep! You won't be so lucky next time!" warns the person on the phone.

"Who the fuck is this? You don't know what you're talking about. Let me ex…," I say before the guy cuts me off.

He speaks in a sinister and almost demented tone before he hangs up, "I don't know where you've been lately, but I'll find you. When I do, it'll be lights out for you. Your days are numbered you raping bastard!"

Connor asks, "Is everything alright dude? What the hell was that about? What's wrong bro?"

"Fucking douche bag! Apparently, it was the fucker who hit me with the pipe. He basically said he's going to kill me next time," I answer angrily.

"What the fuck dude! That's crazy that he has your number. He's probably just trying to scare you. There's no way he knows where you live," Connor interjects.

"Yeah, it's impossible. This place has nothing to do with you, so he won't be coming here. You just have to be more scarce than you already are at your apartment on file. He may be watching," Shannon remarks. "This is so frightening."

"In fact, give me the douche's number and I'll put an end to this shit now. Give me your phone," Connor states.

"Thanks bro, I appreciate that, but my phone won't be any help. He was smart enough to call from a blocked number," I reply.

"Damn, well we can try to have your phone checked and see if the tech people can find out where the call originated from," Shannon offers.

I think that's a good idea, so I tell Shannon and Connor that I'll look into it later. I'd love to find out who this person is before he gets another crack at my life. He may be successful on his next attempt. My life took an unexpected turn, but it's still my life and I value it.

CHAPTER 6

Time is zooming by. Days turn into weeks seemingly overnight. I sometimes wonder where I would be if that rape charge wasn't sent my way. I might be the mayor by now. I'm just kidding. I would have to put in a tremendous amount of work to have such a prestigious position. My mom is still heartbroken over how I fell from grace. One minute I was looking at being a corporate attorney in D.C. and the next minute I was in jail with extremely violent people. That's one hell of a flip.

I'm not in the worst position these days. I have a few bucks saved up and I party like there's no tomorrow. For example, I'm driving Virginia Beach with my girlfriend Emily, Connor, and Shannon for a long weekend. They all ditched work today and we got on the road. The travel distance is only a little more than two hundred miles, so we will be there in no time.

The drive is smooth and very comfortable. We are in Connor's brand spanking new Cadillac Escalade. It's equipped with all the bells and whistles. Sunroof, navigation, heated seats, and TVs in the head rests are just some of the amenities of this vehicle. Connor is definitely living it up! He's even paying for the entire trip. I know this is going to be a rather expensive trip, but Connor wants to treat us to a good time. I'm all for it. It feels good to be associated with people who have good heads on their shoulders and a few dollars in their pockets.

We arrive in Virginia Beach at the condo Connor reserved. Connor walks inside to the attendant to get us checked in. We're unloading our bags from the car when Connor comes back outside and seems a bit disgruntled. His face clearly displays that something is amiss.

"What's wrong?" I ask.

"You know there is always some bullshit getting in the way of a good time. These people are saying that there is a problem with my credit card. I told the lady that I would pay cash, but she stated that policy mandates a credit card be on file for incidentals," Connor narrates.

"It's always something for real. Does that mean we have nowhere to stay?" I ask.

"Well, the room is still reserved, but they need a credit card," Connor replies.

"Oh, if we can use any card, we'll just use

mine," I say.

"Cool. I will give you the cash. They will put a thousand dollar hold on your credit card," says Connor.

"A thousand dollars! Oh, never mind. I don't have that high of a balance on my card," I say reluctantly.

"Here take my card. I have more than enough to cover the charges," Shannon chimes in.

Shannon walks inside to the counter and takes care of the charge. Connor feels embarrassed about the situation and hands Shannon ten crisp one hundred dollar bills. I think he only gave her the money on the spot to save face. He had to let us know without a doubt that it wasn't about the money.

We go to our condo after the paperwork is squared away. When we open the door, all of our mouths drop. The condo is beautiful. The ceilings are cathedral and are about fifteen feet high. There's artwork in here that would make Mona Lisa's smirk turn into a full smile. This condo is full of the comforts fitting of a king. Each bedroom has a master bathroom with a jacuzzi in it. The bed in our room is the softest I've ever sat on and is definitely a California King. Now, I know why there is a thousand dollar hold on Shannon's credit card. This is no Holiday Inn Express. All of the countertops are granite. I know this condo had to set Connor back a pretty penny. If they held a thousand, this place must run at least five thousand.

We all meet back in the common area after we check out the condo. We're all pleased with the space.

"How did you find this place?" asks Shannon.

"It was nothing. Just a little bit of searching on the internet is all. I'm glad you guys like the place. Sorry about the mishap with the card," Connor states.

We all tell Connor the card situation is no big deal. We all share stories about awkward situations we've been in because of our credit or debit cards.

"Okay, okay. Enough of the funny stories. I'm ready to hit the streets. I didn't ride in a car for almost four hours to hear your voices," I say jokingly.

The crew agrees whole-heartedly with me. We agree to be ready for dinner at 7 p.m. We return to our respective bedrooms to iron our clothes, take showers, and get dressed. There's enough time for us to complete all of those things and sneak in a quickie before dinner. Emily and I take full advantage of the extra time. I give her a little preview of what's to come after dinner and a night on the town. It's 7 p.m. sharp and we are heading out the door.

"I don't know what I have a taste for," says Shannon.

"I ate a little before we left the room, but I definitely need to eat some food," I remark.

Emily nudges me in the arm as soon as I finish my sentence. Connor is already laughing because he realizes what I was saying I ate. Shannon eventually gets the joke and begins giggling too. Emily was not laughing at first because she was slightly embarrassed when I initially made the comment, but she is cracking up now. She even jumps in on the joke.

"Well, I'll make sure you eat plenty when we return to the condo. There's plenty of tasty treats over here," Emily retorts.

The car erupts in laughter. Shannon supports Emily one hundred percent on that and so do I. Emily and I make a little wager. We bet that she will make me quit eating her out from not being able to take it before I just get tired.

"Now that's a bet I know I would win," states Connor.

Shannon replies, "I'm willing to bet that you will drown before I stop you. You know I stay wet like a river."

Connor agrees to what she said about being wet. In my mind I agree too. The night we had sex in the car, she was soaking wet. I know not to mention that out loud because things may get very tumultuous. No need to start a riff over nothing. Emily would be livid if she knew I fucked Shannon and she would definitely leave me if she found out about the rape charge. She would probably think that I'm some type of weirdo.

Connor informs us that we need not worry about where to go for dinner. He has made dinner reservations for us at Daniel's Steakhouse and Seafood. I've never heard of the place, but Connor has impeccable taste, so I know there is nothing to worry about. Shannon and Emily have both heard of the place, but have never eaten there before. Each of them has heard that both the food and service are exquisite, so they are full of excitement.

When we arrive at the restaurant, the valet attendant opens our doors and parks the car. The first thing I notice when we walk in is how clean the establishment is. I can see my reflection in the white marble floors of the restaurant and classical music is playing over the sound system.

Shannon says, "I must admit that I am thoroughly impressed. This place is beautiful. The atmosphere is very classy, but not pretentious. It's busy, but not boisterous."

"Yes, I have to agree with Shannon. Great selection so far. Let's see what the food tastes like and how the service is," says Emily.

Daniel's is very exquisite. The hostess greets us by name as soon as we walk in. I don't know how Connor arranged it, but he has done it. Even our waiter knows our names. Connor hasn't had a moment to tell the staff our names, so them learning our names was obviously achieved beforehand. Our ladies are impressed and I am having a great time.

Dinner is delicious and the service is even better. Everything we want is brought to our table before we ask or is delivered in a very prompt fashion. We enjoy fine wine and stimulating conversation. I am thankful for this getaway. Everything is flowing according to plan. The night is bliss.

Everyone in the restaurant can tell that we are having a great time and want to be a part of our night. One guy even tries to insert himself into the fun. He walks past our table and is staring at us. I decide to speak to him because he's glaring so hard.

"Aye, how's it going?" I ask.

"Aye man, it's going," replies the stranger.

I say, "I hear ya. I couldn't help but notice you were glaring over here at us."

"Yeah, sorry about that. Your friend there looks pretty familiar," he reports. "I got up to get a closer look."

"You think I look familiar?" Connor asks eagerly.

"Yeah, buddy. You and I have definitely crossed paths before," he says.

"I beg to differ. I don't know you and you don't know me. Now, please excuse yourself. My friends and I are trying to enjoy our dinner," says Connor.

"That's cold. You shouldn't treat an old friend so coldly. I made you a lot of money," he says.

"I never forget business partners, especially if

you made me a lot of money. You definitely didn't work for me," says Connor.

"I didn't work for you directly…. it was more indirect," says the stranger.

The strange man walks away. He seems to be upset by Connor not knowing who he is. The night is going so smoothly that we don't let some random guy throw us off. We laugh about how foolish that guy is and continue talking about things that actually matter. As soon as we forget about the stranger, we hear a person shouting in our direction.

"I know you, but I don't remember your name. I think you're from up north," says the man.

"I am trying to enjoy a nice night out with my beautiful lady and my friends. You are trying to disrupt that. For the last time, I don't know you and you don't know me. Any simpleton who hears my voice would clearly decipher that I'm a Yankee," Connor replies angrily.

I intervene immediately. I call the waiter over and ask for a manager. This man antagonizing us is ridiculous. He wants to destroy our night. The man is still at our table interrogating Connor. Connor stands up and grabs the man by the collar. Fortunately for the man, the manager and another restaurant employee arrive at our table before Connor could really pummel him. Connor is now upset.

"I hate that I had to grab that guy in front of

you guys. I didn't want it to come to that, but enough is enough. He probably invested with Premier and feels like he knows me. I apologize," Connor says.

Shannon says, "It's cool. That guy was way off base and totally annoying. He would have deserved whatever you gave him baby."

"Dude, I think you're right. He kinda reminds me of that guy from the Fourth of July party we did at Nuno's Pavilion back home, but no need to apologize dude. I was two seconds off of his ass," I say.

Emily states, "I like a little action. I love watching MMA."

Her joke sends the night right back on the course it was on before we digressed. We cap off a great dinner with a fantastic dessert. I imitate Connor grabbing the guy by his collar and add extra things that really didn't happen. We all crack up for the rest of our time at the restaurant. We leave the restaurant and drive to a lounge named Minglers that I looked up. The lounge is dimly lit and the music is soft. It provides an atmosphere that's ideal for dancing and conversing. We take full advantage of what the lounge has to offer. We dance, drink, and laugh the night away.

We arrive back at the condo around 3 a.m. We have all been drinking and are feeling pretty good. I have a buzz that I don't want to ever go away, but I'm drained too. I mention to Emily the bet that she and I made on the way to the restaurant. We both jump in the shower together, so we can get the night jump started. I wash her body and she washes mine. My dick is hard as hell and I can't wait to see who will win the bet. We exit the shower and dry off in the room.

"Where's the wine?" asks Emily.

"Damn, it's in the freezer. I wanted it to be nice and cold for us. I'll go grab it," I say.

When I go into the common area to get to the kitchen where the wine is, I hear moaning and grunting. Shannon and Connor are having sex on the couch. It catches me off guard at first because I really didn't expect to see this happening. They are so ensconced in their sexual activities that they don't even notice me. I am intrigued. I watch for a few seconds and then I proceed to getting the wine. I have my own competition to win.

I go back to our room and receive a pleasant surprise. Emily is standing in the room stark naked with black stilettos on. She has one leg hoisted up on the end table. Emily is fondling her clit when I walk in. I'm aroused instantly, but I don't make a move toward her. Instead, I sip some of the wine directly out of the bottle and enjoy Emily's show. As she caresses her clit with one hand, she motions me over to her with her other hand. I immediately walk over to her. Emily removes the bottle from my mouth and inserts the finger she was playing with herself with into my mouth. I suck her finger as she sips from the wine bottle.

She sits the bottle down and we share a long passionate kiss. I lick Emily down her neck as she strokes my hard dick. I grab my dick at its base and rub it on Emily's pussy. She moans erotically with every stroke of my dick on her pussy. I feel her juices spilling all over my dick. Emily's breathing gets heavier as she begins to gyrate on my dick.

"Put it in," she orders while panting.

I'm teasing her, so I don't comply. I continue massaging my dick on her clit. Emily raises her leg back up on the night stand as she slowly and seductively leans over. She's at a perfect angle for me to stick my hard shaft in her wet hot box. I stick my dick in her pussy. When she feels my dick inside of her, she lets out an "aah" to signify she loves the way my dick feels inside of her. She looks back at me while I stroke her from behind. She's biting her lips and pinching her nipples as I jab her repeatedly.

"Yes, Alex!" she screams. "Go deeper!"

Emily is pushing her booty back on me as I'm pushing my dick into her. Her legs begin to shake as the smell of fuck fills the air. The room is filled with moans, oohs, and aahs. Her pussy is so wet that my dick going in and out of her starts to sounds like waves splashing in the ocean. I pull my dick out of her and pussy juices are dripping from my dick.

Emily looks back to see why I stopped and sees her juices all over my dick. She turns around and begins sucking her juices off my dick. She protrudes her tongue out and runs it on my ball sack. She licks my balls and continues all the way up to the head of my dick. Her mouth feels so good that I can barely stand up. My knees want to buckle at every motion she makes. Emily looks my dick in the eye and spits on it. She inserts my dick into her mouth and sucks it again. She attempts to put my entire cock in her mouth, but she is unable to. She almost chokes on it. When she pulls her mouth off my dick, there's a long line of spit on it.

I pick Emily up and throw her on the bed. I drizzle some of the wine on her supple breasts and slowly begin to lick it down her stomach to her pussy. Emily begins to groan as I swirl my tongue on her clit. Her pussy gets wetter and wetter with every stroke of my tongue. I stick my tongue inside her pussy and lick her G-spot. While I'm eating her pussy, I gently rub her asshole like I'm polishing a quarter. Emily's never felt this sensation before, but I can tell by the way she's reacting that she likes it.

I lick Emily's inner thigh on one leg then kiss her pussy subtly and then let me lips lead to her other inner thigh. She locks her legs around my neck and all I can do is lock my face on to her juicy peach. Emily spreads her legs like she's about to do a split, so I take the opportunity to catch my breath.

"Put your dick back inside of me. I want to cum on your dick," she says.

I get off the bed and walk over to a chair in the room. I sit down in the chair and begin stroking my dick. Emily grabs a bottle of edible oil off of the nightstand and struts over to where I'm seated. She takes over stroking my dick and starts giving him subtle kisses. She squirts the oil on my soldier and dives in like it's an ice cream cone. She starts at the base near my balls and extends her tongue and slides it around the circumference of my pole. The heat and moisture from her mouth blankets my dick and sends a tingling sensation through my body. I wrap her hair around my hand and slowly guide her head as I fuck her mouth. She winds her head as she sucks my dick like she's trying to loosen a sore spot in her neck.

I'm ready to feel Emily's wet walls, so I let her hair go and direct her to sit on my dick. Emily mounts me as I sit. She slides up and down my dick wildly as she screams. Her hair is flopping around as if the wind is blowing it. My lap is drenched as Emily's juices pour down my shaft and balls onto my lap. Her titties jiggle up and down as she pounces on my slong.

"You like that?" she asks. "Does she feel good to you?"

I'm so taken away by the pleasure of her pussy that I can't muster a verbal response. I simply nod my head at Emily. Sweat is running down her face and burning her eyes, but she doesn't stop riding my dick. I grab hold of her ass while I enjoy the ride. Emily's breathing heavily and sweating profusely, so I know she's tired.

I wipe the perspiration from her brow as I say, "Let me take over."

Emily gets up to grab the bottle of wine and rushes back to me as I'm standing up. To my shock, Emily knocks me back down in the chair and sits on my lap facing away from me. I spread her legs open and nuzzle her clit. She turns her face to give me a kiss, so I lean forward. She sucks my bottom lip and kisses me softly like only she can. Her lips are juicy, but her pussy lips are even juicer. Emily stands up and pours the oil on my dick again.

She grabs my dick and holds it at an angle while she starts to sit back down again. Only this time it's different. She isn't moving as swiftly and wildly as she was before. This time she's more calculated and methodical. She's angling my dick towards her asshole. The head of my dick meets her asshole, but it's very tight. After a minute of trying, my dick finally enters her ass. Emily's body is tense as she slides down my pipe of pleasure. I grip Emily's hips as I guide her down.

"Ooh, it feels so good in my ass! I love it," Emily utters.

Finally my entire dick is stuffed into her ass and she's enjoying every inch of it. She lifts herself up and lets herself down slowly like a hydraulic lift. Her ass is so tight that it feels like my dick is being squeezed by compression sleeve. I know I'm going to cum in her ass at any moment. Emily reaches down and fondles my balls and tickles my perineum. My dick gets harder from the additional stimulation. Emily's tension goes away and now she's thoroughly enjoying getting fucked in the ass.

"Go faster!" I order.

"Yes daddy!" she answers.

Emily leans forward and braces her hands on her knees while my dick is still in her ass and starts jerking up and down on my dick. I start slapping her ass to the point where it's turning red. Emily looks back at me and starts slapping her ass with me. She speeds up the intensity of her jockeying on my dick. She's smoothing her hand over her clit and starts moaning and screaming as she spasms as if she's in an epileptic fit. I feel her getting weak and about to fall to the floor, so I grab her by the waist and stand up. I take command and start fucking her in the ass with short jab strokes. Each jab stoke I give her sends more sensation to the tip of my dick. Emily releases a short scream with each poke I give her and they're turning me on even more. I give Emily a stroke of my entire dick in her ass and her short yells turn into a sustained high pitch like she's a soprano singer. Now, she's incessantly screaming at the top of her lungs. My strokes become more violent and powerful as I release a massive amount of cum in her ass.

CHAPTER 7

The worst thing about going on vacation is that the vacation seems to end overnight. The weekend in Virginia is a week behind us now. I had a really good time hanging with Emily, Connor, and Shannon. I know I had a great time because I needed a vacation from the vacation. I'm more drained now than I was before we left for Virginia Beach. I'm not complaining though. I would do it all over again tomorrow if I had the chance. The Crew, as we call ourselves, is planning another trip to Las Vegas in the next couple of months.

I know my friends and associates would be extremely jealous of me if I could post pictures of the trip to Virginia. I wanted to post the pictures of all of us on Facebook and Instagram, but I couldn't because I'm on parole and didn't get clearance to leave the state. I'm sure that our photos from the weekend would have received more likes than I ever could imagine they would. I know we were looking good and having fun, but it seemed to be on another level based on all the attention we received at the beach. Emily and I were battling Connor and Shannon for best looking couple. In my opinion, the competition wasn't even close. We blew Connor and Shannon away like a tornado blows leaves. I'm looking forward to many more memorable moments.

This week is slow for me as far as work is concerned. I only have to work on some business cards for Premier and other little odds and ends. I'm glad the week didn't start off like a NASCAR race because I was tired from the trip, but now I'm ready to do some work. I've never been the type of person who enjoys sitting idly. My mind is always spinning and processing the next move. Fortunately, I receive a call from Shannon letting me know she's bringing me some work. I tell her that I would meet her somewhere just to have a reason to leave the apartment, but she insists on coming to my place. I guess she's still being cautious about being seen with me in D.C.

While I'm awaiting Shannon's arrival, someone begins knocking on my door. The only person I'm expecting today is Shannon, but she's not due here until later today. The only people who know I live here are Shannon, Emily, and Connor. I'm almost afraid to answer the door because it could be my parole officer. My mind is racing out of control. If it's my parole officer, he'll violate me for not letting him know I have another place to live. I can't go back to jail. No fucking way! How did he find out when nobody knows I live here? I don't even receive mail here. The only mail that comes here is for Connor pertaining to Premier Investments. I grab a knife out of the kitchen to protect myself if I have to. For all I know, it could be the same person who attacked me. He could've found my new residence.

There's another knock at the door. I ease over to the window to see if there are any cops or cars I don't recognize out there. There is a brand new black Mercedes Benz parked out front. I've never seen that car a day in my life. I may be over exaggerating this situation. The person knocking at the door probably isn't even looking for me. They're most likely at the wrong address. I will just sit here quietly and wait for the unknown visitor to depart. Just as my nerves calm and I accept the fact that the person knocking at the door isn't looking for me, I hear a soft voice calling my name. I don't respond because I was unable to decipher whose voice it is. Next, I see what looks like a file folder being slid under the door. I don't immediately move for it because it may be a setup. After a minute, I am pretty sure that the folder is from Shannon. That is the same style folder she normally brings work for me in.

I decide to inconspicuously look out the window to see if I can learn the package dropper's identity. The woman appears in my line of sight from the window and my suspicions are confirmed. It is Shannon. She is walking toward the black Benz. She must have gotten a new car. Her taste is superb.

"Shannon," I call from the window. "I'm opening the door now."

She immediately looks up at me when I call her name and starts for the door again. I unlock the door and she comes inside.

"What are you hiding from?" Shannon asks. "I'm hiding from my parole officer or the guy who's trying to kill me. I didn't know who was knocking at the door. You could have been anyone," I say.

Shannon responds, "I understand that. I called your name too because I figured something like that was the case."

I respond, "I heard my name, but your voice was too low for me to make out who it was. I see somebody has some new slick wheels."

"Yes! I love it too. Your best bud Connor bought it for me! I'm surprised he didn't tell you about it," Shannon replies. "I'll pull into the garage, so you can check it out."

She walks outside to the car and pulls into the garage. It's a great looking car. I know Connor paid a king's ransom for this fine automobile. It's top of the line all the way. He spoke of getting Shannon a gift that would really impress her and seal the deal, but I had no idea he'd purchase such an ostentatious gift. He always gets the job done.

We stay in the garage briefly looking at the car and then I direct Shannon back into the house. Shannon and I discuss the details of what she needs research on. It appears this client is extra important because she offers to pay me one and a half times more than what she normally pays me.

I'm the right man for the job. Between the internet and the law library, I will find exactly what she needs and put it together for her. Shannon departs after our conversation to head back to work and I get to work. After a few hours of work, I call Connor to let him tell me about the purchase of the vehicle.

I say, "Nice ride! Business must really be booming!"

Connor replies, "Hey bud, you know first-hand how things are going."

I say, "Yeah, things are going according to the plan. Money is rolling in. Business is great! That Benz is sweet bro!"

"Thanks. Shannon deserves it!" says Connor.

Connor and I speak briefly. We both have work to do. The life of a businessman can be very demanding at times. I have to be diligent in completing my assignments. If I'm not on point in handling my affairs, I will not succeed in my endeavors.

I was so wrapped up in my duties that I didn't realize that my phone had died. I guess it's best it went dead because I was able to work uninterrupted. I'm sure Emily is looking for me by now. We haven't spoken since last night. I put my phone on the charger and immediately hit the power button. After the phone boots up, the message alert begins to beep over and over again. I'm receiving countless voicemails and text messages. I cannot check one message without another message interrupting me. Something extremely vile must be going on.

I finally open one text message without another one coming through. Shannon wants me to text her as soon as possible. She claims the matter is extremely urgent. I know something is wrong because she wouldn't have texted me so many times if it wasn't serious. I hope nothing is wrong with Connor. Someone could have seen us together and harmed him because of my sex offender status. I would never forgive myself if something happened to him because of my conviction even though it's not really my fault. Maybe I should just blame Shannon; it's really all of her doing anyway.

I should be ashamed of myself for jumping to conclusions. The best bet is for me to call Shannon to see what the matter is.

Unfortunately, she doesn't answer the phone when I call. I check my voicemail messages to see if I can get a better understanding of what's going on. The first voicemail I listen to is of Shannon crying and trying to explain what's going on, but her voice is too muffled for me to make out what she's saying. There are more sniffles in the message than anything.

The second voicemail has a different tone. Shannon's tone is now one of anger and frustration. She has the voice of someone who is agitated because her calls are being ignored. She is also screaming at the top of her lungs. What could have transpired in such a short period of time that has impacted her so deeply? She was just jovial and upbeat earlier today. Now, she's on my voicemail weeping and screaming. I hope she calls back because she has me flustered.

I call Connor to see if he has any input on the matter, but he doesn't know anything either. He hasn't heard from Shannon via text or phone call. I think to myself how strange that is that she has not called him. I neglect to tell Connor that Shannon was clearly disturbed on my voicemail. I don't want to cause him any distress, especially since I don't know what's really going on. I merely tell him I had a question for Shannon pertaining to some work I'm doing for her and that the work is time sensitive. Finally, after what seems to be a year, Shannon calls me back. I eagerly answer her phone call.

"Shannon, I am glad you called back. I heard your voicemails, but couldn't make them out," I say.

"I know. I was a mess earlier when I called. I apologize," Shannon says.

"It's cool. But what's going on? What's wrong? Did I make a mistake with some research I did for you?" I ask.

"I know I had your mind going through roller coaster loops. Again, I'm sorry for that. My problem is work related, but it isn't anything you did or did not do. It actually has nothing to do with you, but I need your help," Shannon narrates.

I reply, "Tell me what I can do to help and if I can assist, I will."

Shannon proceeds to tell me how her problem is work related. According to Shannon, the company she works for lost a three million dollar block of business today. She reports that her firm is not taking this lightly. She's taking the three million dollar loss hard because it was an account that she was in charge of. She was pivotal in bringing those clients on board and keeping them happy. Shannon feels that she let her company down.

She tells me that she's frustrated because there is nothing she can do to bring the client back to the firm. The clients are adamant about not returning to them. She's also frustrated because of what the client reported. The client stated that they didn't want to do business with the firm anymore because they received reports that

Shannon's company is employing people who have unsound business practices. Her clients were afraid that they would suffer severe losses if they didn't cut ties immediately. Shannon is further irritated because the clients are firm in their decision. According to Shannon, the client stated that they didn't know the identity of the displeasing employee.

I say, "I totally understand why you are upset. Three million dollars' worth of business is no chump change. Sorry, you have to go through this. I'm sure some heads will roll because of this situation."

Shannon replies, "Thanks. You're right. My employers are beyond livid at this situation. I'm angry too. I worked my ass off to win that account only for it to be snatched from me for something I didn't do."

I verbalize, "I'd be kicking doors down and flipping desks over if I were you. Just kidding of course. I'd be really angry though."

"All because of some idiot. I bet the culprit works on the second floor in the mailroom. Those people down there always look like they're up to something," comments Shannon.

I ask, "How is your company responding? Are they considering getting rid of you?"

Shannon states, "No, they're not considering removing me, thank God. They know it's not my fault, but they asked me to see if I can get to the bottom of this fiasco."

"Well, that's great! At least they're level headed. It would suck for you to take the fall for something that's out of your hands," I speak.

"Yeah, they've been great about it towards me. I volunteered to take lead on this situation because it directly affects me," states Shannon.

"I wouldn't expect anything different from you. Take the bull by the horns. Way to go," I utter.

"You're such a cheerleader," Shannon retorts.

"Haha, oh you have jokes? You mentioned needing my help; what can I help with?" I ask.

"Yes, I totally need your help. Probably more now than ever before. I need you to get as much information as possible on every employee here at the firm," answers Shannon.

"Shannon, do you realize how much work and time would be required to complete such a task?" I ask.

Shannon replies, "I know this is quite a cumbersome task, but it has to be done. This is of the utmost importance. Alex, you always could find any information if it was out there. That's why I hired you to begin with. You're the best."

"I get that. I really understand that you want to get to the bottom of this, but it's just a lot of work. To be honest, there's no way for me to complete the other work you gave me today and be able to take on this task as well. I'm just being straight with you," I explain.

Shannon clearly doesn't like my response, but she understands. We come to an agreement that she will acquire the work she gave me earlier and I will assume this new task of searching through employee records. Since she doesn't have the three million dollar account, she has more time in her schedule, but she still needs to be available to keep all other client relationships in good standing.

I tell Shannon that I'm on board fully with helping her through such a troubling time. She informs me that money is no object when it comes to me researching the staff at the firm. According to Shannon, the firm is backing the investigation financially, so I will be paid handsomely. I'm all for being well compensated. The American Dream is to make a lot of money and be prosperous. I'll play my part in achieving the dream.

"Bring me the information and I'll get right to it," I comment.

"Cool, let me go. I have to go to Human Resources and get all of these employee files together," Shannon says. "Thanks again for being willing to help and being flexible. I know I can be a bit demanding at times."

"No problem. I don't think you're demanding. Working for you has been a pleasure and very rewarding both financially and intrinsically to say the least," I narrate.

"Thanks, for not making me out to be a witch.

I appreciate it," replies Shannon.

"My comments were sincere; you really aren't difficult to work with. I do have a suggestion about this upcoming research I have to do. Maybe break the files up into bits and pieces. I'd rather not have a million files sitting in here at once," I voice.

"Ok, what do you have in mind for the work?" Shannon inquires.

I tell Shannon that I want the files to be separated according to the alphabet. I inform her to bring me the employee records that start with the first four letters of the alphabet. I will be able to manage those files much better than all at one time. When I have cleared the first set of employees, she's to bring me the files for the employee last names that correspond with the next letters of the alphabet. I know she wants this information in a timely fashion, but this will be a slow and grueling process. I may even need to hire a private investigator. Fortunately, the firm isn't extremely large, so there aren't thousands of people to investigate. I pride myself in being thorough and meticulous in all things I do. I am not willing to compromise the integrity of my work just to please Shannon. Speed doesn't always translate to accuracy. My mom always told me, "If you're going to do it, do it right." Her teachings still apply to this day.

CHAPTER 8

It has been a month since Shannon asked me to look into the personal lives of all employees at Mullins and Philbert. This is a daunting task to say the least. I was really up for the challenge when she initially asked, but this duty has become a bit overwhelming. I have delved into the personal lives of all employees ranging from the custodial staff, maintenance staff, and interns. Unfortunately, none of my queries have been fruitful. Without anyone knowing, I've even investigated the partners of the firm and found nothing remotely out of place. The most incriminating information I was able to find was that an employee in the mailroom is breaking the law by driving back and forth to work while on a suspended license. That definitely doesn't constitute a reason for a client to jump ship because they don't trust the integrity of the firm's employees.

To make matters worse, Shannon's employers are looking for answers yesterday. They are looking for accountability. Understandably, they're not willing to sweep a three million dollar loss under the rug. Also, they know how this type of scandal could snowball into something even bigger than a client taking its business elsewhere. The firm's executives are worried about this information being spread and other clients finding out about it. There could be a mass exodus of customers with accounts even larger than the one they already lost.

Shannon's firm has paid me a pretty penny to find answers and I have been unable to deliver anything promising. I feel bad because her neck is on the line and I can't help her out of the jam she's in. I almost feel like I'm stealing from the firm. Maybe I should just give them their money back if I don't find anything. I'm always able to find the information that I seek. What am I missing? Where am I not looking? I'll figure it out.

Shannon knocks at the door. She is pushing through the door as soon as she hears the lock unfastened. She's been pretty unsettled and on a war path ever since she lost that block of business.

Shannon says directly, "I'm not here for small talk. I need results and you're not producing!"

"I cannot find what's not there. I've looked

through every employee's life inside and out. Maybe your client parted ways because he or she didn't want to do business with your company anymore. They could have used this fictitious story to throw everyone off of their true motives," I say.

"I never considered that side of the situation. That's a lot to go through just to end business with us. It can't be that simple. Even if it is, there is no way my employers will buy this tale. They want conclusive facts not opinions," Shannon states.

I reply, "You have to sell them on it. Look at it from my point of view. I've always been able to find whatever information there is to be found. You have to find it strange that all of a sudden I can't find out some simple information about an employee who isn't living right. Shannon, use your common sense. You know that research is my thing. I could find Jimmy Hoffa if someone put me up to it."

"Yeah, you make a great point. I asked for your help on this because you have always been able to deliver. I had many other options to exhaust, but I chose you. You're the information ferret. I don't know how well they'll take this information. I'm gonna hate having to tell them no viable leads have been discovered," Shannon says in a frustrated manner.

"It may be hard for your employers to accept, but they may just have to. If you have files of former employees, I can look into them if you want. I'm trying to remain optimistic about finding a lead, but it's not looking good," I reply.

Shannon responds, "I'll get you the records of former employees. Please keep searching. It really means a lot. Thanks a million. I'm heading to the office to speak with my employers."

Shannon goes to work and reports to her superiors all the details of the investigation. She proposes to the firm the idea of the client just wanting to part ways with them. She tells them how strange it is that the client broke ties with their company with no evidence at all and couldn't provide a name of the employee who caused them to leave. The heads of the firm aren't pleased with her findings, but they have no choice, but to accept the bad news. They know that Shannon's work at the firm is flawless and feel that if she can't uncover the truth then nobody else can either. They urge Shannon to keep on with her investigation and to keep them apprised of any new details.

Business gets back to normal at the firm for Shannon. Her employers have moved on from the large account being lost. Shannon was able to recruit more clients to replace what was missing and no other clients have left the firm because of this phantom mischievous employee. Everything is as it used to be. Shannon instructs me to stop my review of employees' records and gives me a file to prepare like normal.

I'm glad things have calmed down at her firm because Shannon wasn't handling the stress very well. She was nothing close to her normal friendly self. She was all business and no play. Even Connor noticed a big difference in her personality over the last few weeks. Not that I blame her, she was tasked with a cumbersome job that meant a lot to her professionally. We all have been stressed by something at one point or another. I can remember a few times during college, so I can't blame Shannon. I'm sure I was aggravating to some of my friends back then. Connor and I both agree that we will give her a pass for her grizzly bear like behavior.

Connor and I also discuss the Vegas trip that's long overdue. Connor and Emily have wanted this trip for a while now, but Shannon and I couldn't make it happen because of the scandal at her job. Now that the tension is alleviated, it's time for a Vegas run. Hopefully, Shannon is in favor of a stress relieving weekend in Sin City. I know for damn sure I'm ready. We're confident that Shannon's ready to go too.

There's no way Shannon will turn down this trip. Only an idiot would refuse a free trip to the entertainment mecca of the world. Besides that, she always spoke of going to Vegas when we attended law school. Visiting Las Vegas is definitely on her bucket list. I don't blame her. I've always wanted to visit Vegas myself.

I've heard countless stories of how much fun

it is. According to all the reports I've heard, a Vegas night is one that a person will never forget. What happens in Vegas, stays in Vegas!

I'm stoked about going over to Sin City. To be honest, I'm tired of hearing everyone else's stories about Las Vegas and I'm ready to have my own narratives to share. All of the movies that have been set in Vegas make going to the desert town seem overwhelmingly glamorous and like there's no other place to be.

They say the lights on all the casinos at night are jaw dropping and awe inspiring. I'm so ready to go. In fact, even if Shannon doesn't want to go, I'm still taking Emily. There will be no need to let Shannon and Connor preclude us from having a dream vacation.

Connor contacts Shannon via video chat. She picks up and the image of her pops up on the iPad screen. She's smiling from ear to ear. All you see is her pearly white teeth illuminating in the connection.

Connor states, "Hi, honey. Seeing your face just made my day."

"You are too sweet. I don't deserve you. You just made my day with your kind words," Shannon replies.

I'm sitting here listening to their conversation and it's about to make me throw up from all this sweet and sensitive talk. Connor knows I don't want to hear all of this mushy conversation. Although, he knows I don't like it, he continues anyway. I think he really wants to see me cough up the contents of my stomach.

"Yes, you do deserve me and I deserve you. We're together because we deserve each other," Connor states.

A tear trickles down Shannon's cheek. I know she's about to reply with some overly sensitive comment that I don't need or care to hear. Before she replies, I chime in.

"You two are disgusting. I can't take any more of this. You two should just get together and whisper sweet nothings to each other all night. To be in love is one thing, but this sappy display of affection is too much for me," I say.

They both burst out laughing. I start laughing too. I guess my comments were funny, but I didn't intend for them to be. I just wanted to get them to shut up.

Shannon states, "I didn't know you were with my sweetheart. I would've spared you my sweet comments. Sweetie, I'm impressed. You expressed your feelings for me openly in front of Alex. Now, that's true love."

I think I should've kept my mouth shut. I made this conversation even worse. I hope he just gets to the point.

"Hi, Alex. Don't be jealous because we have a good thing going. You should be happy for us," Shannon says jokingly.

I reply, "You know I'm your number one advocate. You two could give someone instant diabetes with all this sweet talk. Connor, get to the point of the call is all I'm saying."

Shannon asks, "What's the point of the call? What's going on? Is everything okay?"

"Everything's fine. Just need to run something by you," Connor replies.

"Well, you have my attention. Shoot whenever you're ready," says Shannon.

Connor asks Shannon if she would be able to take the trip to Las Vegas leaving in the middle of next week. His presentation to convince her to go is flawless. He knows exactly what to say to Shannon to get her on board. He details where we'll be staying as well as an itinerary of what we're going to do while there.

Shannon is enthusiastic about the trip and says she will not miss it for the world. However, she says that she won't be able to leave until Friday of next week. I'm glad she can make the trip because she needs to relax. She has been working double time since she lost the client at the firm. Hopefully, this Vegas trip will help her blood pressure go back to normal. This will be a fantastic way for her to get things completely back on track. I'm excited to say the least. The trip is set.

Seemingly as fast as we booked the Vegas trip, the day of Connor's and my departure is here. We have to make a road trip of it because I'm still on parole and I wasn't granted permission to leave the area. It's a long drive, but it's cool because Connor and I love road trips. Emily wasn't as enthusiastic as Connor and I were about taking a super long drive, so she opted to fly out on Friday with Shannon. I don't blame her and to be honest, there is no need for her to drive all the way across the country with us. Emily stayed the night with me at my place last night, so she could receive some pre-Vegas activity. Shannon and Connor both spent the night here too. Shannon came over late last night after she finished entertaining some clients because she wanted to see Connor before our departure. Emily and I were already in my room when she arrived, so we didn't see her last night. I'm in the kitchen making a light breakfast when Connor joins me.

"What's up bud? Almost ready to hit the road?" I inquire.

"Oh, yeah! I'm ready whenever you are. I slept great and I'm very well rested," Connor replies.

I voice sarcastically, "I bet you are! And I'm sure Shannon is too! Go get her. Emily wants to see her."

"I'm not going to get her. She's fussy in the morning. Dude, I had to get away from her. I'm not out here with you for your looks," Connor jokes.

I send Shannon a text to come to the kitchen, stop being lazy, and to get up because Emily wants to see her. Emily and I are both sitting in the kitchen eating when Shannon walks in.

"Hi, Emily," says Shannon.

"Hey, it's been too long," remarks Emily as she gets up and hugs Shannon.

"I know. It seems like it's been forever. It really hasn't been that long though," states Shannon.

Emily asks, "How have you been? What's new?"

"I've been busy as hell to say the least. Work has me stressed out of my mind. I have some new clients at work, but other than that everything is pretty much the same," answers Shannon.

Emily replies, "Unfortunately, I know exactly what you mean about being stressed at work. I think I've aged a little since the last time we saw each other."

"Stress this and stress that. We're days away from being in the entertainment capital of the world and all you two can do is talk about work and stress. You two are killing my good spirit," I say.

"Let us have our girl talk. Close your ears and you won't have to hear what we're saying," says Shannon.

Emily and Shannon both tell me to mind my business. They gang up on me and talk trash. I can exchange puns with them all day if I have to. I'm a lawyer at heart and a very formidable adversary for anyone who wants to challenge me.

"If you close your mouth, I won't have to hear you either," I respond.

Emily states, "Alex, that's rude. Apologize to her. That was very insensitive of you."

Emily hits me with a potato square that was on her plate. Emily is not as thick skinned as Shannon is. I apologize to Shannon even though I don't have to. Shannon's not the least bit phased by my joke. She knows it wasn't harsh and only in the friendly spirit of the joke.

"You know you didn't have to say sorry," verbalizes Shannon. "That was nothing. Emily's making you soft. Way to break him down girl."

"Call me soft if you want, but I wasn't the one talking about being stressed out at work. That was definitely you two," I speak.

"Don't start again," orders Shannon.

Emily asks, "Do I have to hit you with another potato?"

"No, you definitely don't need to hit me with another potato or anything else. What you both need to do is leave all the stress and work talk here and party like there's no tomorrow when we get to Las Vegas," I dictate.

"I don't know about Emily, but I can and will surely follow those instructions," Shannon offers jokingly.

Emily chimes in, "That sounds like something I can do too."

"Great, Emily. I have an entire set of instructions I want you to follow once we arrive in our hotel room," I say while licking my lips erotically.

"You are so bad," suggests Emily as she winks at me seductively.

"We have to get there before any hanky panky happens," vocalizes Shannon.

"You got that right. We need to get on the road if we're gonna be there by the time you and Shannon arrive. Connor, I made the breakfast, so you have to load our bags into the car," I say.

"I think you're a douche, but I'll still load the bags. Besides, I don't want you scratching my car up," Connor replies as he grabs a bag to take to the car.

Emily states, "Well, since you made breakfast, I'll load the dishwasher."

Shannon helps Emily with the dishes and I go to my room to ensure I'm not leaving anything behind. After a thorough looking over, I'm comfortable that I didn't forget anything. Emily walks back in the room and we chat.

"You didn't have to come back in here to keep me company. You haven't seen Shannon in quite some time, I would've understood if you two caught up for a while," I verbalize.

Emily replies, "It's cool. Shannon had to start getting ready for work, so she hopped in the shower. I figured I'd come see your handsome face for a few more minutes before you go."

I hear the car trunk slam shut, so I look out of the window. Connor is outside and the car is all loaded up.

I yell out the window, "Hey bud. I'll be down in a minute. I hope you know that I'm driving the first leg."

Connor stays true to form and doesn't reply. Instead, he shoots me both middle fingers and begins laughing. Eventually, Shannon goes down to keep him company. I stay upstairs with Emily to make sure she knows to lock up the house when she departs. Additionally, I complete one more check. I abhor leaving things behind when I'm going places. I end up having to buy whatever it is that I left behind when I get to my destination.

I have everything I need, so I kiss Emily goodbye and I walk downstairs and jump in the car. Connor makes a comment about having to load all of the luggage into the car. He knows loading the luggage in the car wasn't an even trade with me having made breakfast.

"Thanks for letting me load the luggage for you," Connor states humorously.

"I reply, "It was part of the plan."

We all laugh at Connor because we know I set him up to load the luggage. Better him to load the luggage than me. Not that it was a lot, but I rather not have done it. Besides, I'm driving the first leg of our road trip. I need to conserve my energy. It's a fair tradeoff. Well, at least I think.

Connor and Shannon say their goodbyes and we pull off after she gives him a long passionate kiss while leaning in the passenger's window. Connor and I have taken plenty of road trips before, but this will be the longest one by far. When I was a freshman in college, Connor and I drove from our hometown of Linden, New Jersey all the way to Miami, Florida to partake in Memorial Day festivities. The road trip was phenomenal and the time spent on South Beach was fantastic too. Ever since then, we've been hooked on taking road trips. I hope this trip is as fun and memorable as the others we've taken. For the most part, the drive is a straight shot across the country.

Our trip to Vegas is smooth and seamless. We arrive in Las Vegas at 3 p.m. on Friday afternoon. We got here before Shannon and Emily, so we have to pick them up from the airport. Instead of driving around to burn time, we decide to go to the hotel and steal a nap until it's time to go get them. At 5 p.m., I get a call from Emily stating that she and Shannon have just landed and are on their way to baggage claims to get their luggage. I tell her that Connor and I are on our way to get them.

We arrive at the airport just as Emily and Shannon are walking outside. Connor nearly sleeps on the horn to get their attention, but they're completely oblivious to his efforts. I call Emily and tell her that we're in the white Tahoe and to come get in the car. They both walk over to the vehicle. They both are confused as to why we're in a Tahoe.

"Connor, what's with the new car? Did you buy another car when you two got here?" Shannon inquires.

"No, that's not the case. I wouldn't buy this gas guzzler out here to have to drive it back to D.C. We had a little trouble with one of the tires, but nothing major. The shop has the car," Connor explains.

"Oh well, I'm glad you guys made it okay! I would be dead tired if I were you," Shannon comments.

We load their luggage and head back to the hotel. We get to the hotel in no time and get settled in.

"I must admit that this hotel is kick ass! I can't honestly say that I've ever been in such a luxurious place before. This makes the hotel in Virginia look like a dump," I say to The Crew.

"I totally agree," says Emily. "This place had to cost a small fortune. I think I could die here. In fact, I know I could die here."

Shannon replies, "It is an exquisite space, but I don't know about dying here. However, I know I could live here. This place is fit for a queen and I am that."

We are on the top floor of the Wynn hotel. Our room is huge. The apartment I grew up in on Middlesex Street is less than half the size of this place. I would be happy just staying in this room for the entire time we are here. It's just that nice.

I know better than to offer that idea to The Crew because they might jump me for suggesting something so absurd.

Honestly, I really want to find out if all the hype about Las Vegas is true. Connor is the one who planned every detail of this getaway. I'm sure we'll be completely satisfied with whatever he has in store for us. He's visited here before on many occasions, so he has all of the proper contacts and knows the best places to go.

"We have things to do and places to see! We have a show to catch that starts in 45 minutes. Chop, chop. Let's get showered up, dressed, and out the door," says Connor.

Shannon replies, "I know not to ask where we're going because you aren't going to tell me. You're always so secretive. If you tell me where we're going, it won't spoil the surprise for me."

"You'll find out when we arrive. I want you guys to wonder what we are going to see up until the very last moment. It's better that way. Trust me," Connor shoots back.

Emily asks, "Can we at least know what type of show it is?"

"Now why would I tell you that?" asks Connor.

Shannon cuts in and says, "So we can put the appropriate outfits on. I would hate to be dressed formally and we are going to a rodeo. That wouldn't be sexy at all."

"Alright, I see your point. We are going to Cirque de Soleil," Connor replies.

Emily replies, "I hear those shows are the best. I've wanted to catch one of their shows for years now. I'm excited!"

Emily tells me every other month about her desire to catch one of those shows. Going to the show first will set the tone for the trip. I know Emily will be in a great mood for the rest of the getaway. In one mini vacation, she'll be able to scratch two things off her life's to do list. I'm happy just to be away from D.C. and with the people I care about. I really think Shannon is going to get the most out of this trip. This trip will allow her to let it all hang out. She has been a slave to work lately. Hopefully, she'll return home refreshed and invigorated. As for Connor, he's good no matter where he is. He just floats around handling affairs for Premier and is pretty happy go lucky. Nothing bothers him, so this trip is all for Shannon.

We freshen up and make it to the show right on time. Emily has never gotten ready for anything that fast in her life. She normally needs three hours to get herself ready. She has set a new record today. I will hold this against her in the future. I no longer want to hear anything about beauty takes time. That's her favorite line whenever I put pressure on her to get dressed and ready to go quickly. Even though I rush her, I actually don't mind Emily taking her time because she always looks beautiful when she finishes.

The line is long, but is well managed. We have front row seats and feel like we are part of the show because we are so close. The show is filled with flames, acrobatic stunts, and death defying maneuvers. I feel like at any moment someone from the show could jump off the stage into my lap. The cast of the show is obviously well trained because they're completely in sync and perform the stunts effortlessly.

After the show, we decide to walk down the Strip. Words can't accurately express how electric the strip is. This is one place you just have to visit to fully understand. The strip is so bright from all of the flashing lights that I need my sunglasses on. I would fit right in because hundreds of people have their shades on too. The streets are riddled with people performing on the sidewalks for money. Some of the performances are excellent. They're so good that you would think they're professionals who didn't get a big break. Of all the shows that I've seen outdoors, I think the water show in front of the Bellagio has to be the best. It is absolutely breathtaking.

We decide to vacate Las Vegas Blvd. for a little while and go inside the casinos to do some gambling. I'm a Black Jack and Roulette man, so I'm going to head straight for those tables. Connor doesn't like the idea of gambling away money that he worked so hard for, therefore he doesn't play anything. He just plans to keep me company and makes suggestions while I play the games. The ladies don't know anything about card games or Roulette, so they plan to play the slot machines. I wouldn't mind them sticking around, but I really don't want them to be in the way of what I'm trying to do. Fortunately, they don't care about watching me play and I'm cool with that. As we walk toward the casino, we hand them some cash and they disappear instantaneously.

"Before you ladies go, what numbers should I put my money on?" I ask.

Emily states, "Seven is my lucky number, so I think you should play that number."

"I'll be sure to put some money on seven," I say.

"Well, eleven has always been lucky for me. My parent's anniversary is on the eleventh of July and my niece was born in November. Can't lose with eleven," dictates Shannon.

I let out a slight chuckle and say, "Seven eleven, just like the convenience store. Works for me. See you ladies later. We have business to handle."

Two hours later, we meet back up with the girls on the strip. They've been winning and losing back and forth with the money we gave them to gamble with. They pretty much broke even on the slot machines. The first time I ever played a slot machine I broke even. Surprisingly, I had plenty of fun while doing so. I was in a casino in Atlantic City and only had twenty bucks to play with, but the twenty dollars lasted me all night. Every time I got down to my last few quarters I won more money. It was battle of man and machine and I refused to lose. Even though I broke even, I felt like I won because I was entertained all night and didn't lose a dime.

"How'd you guys make out on the tables?" Emily asks.

"Great!" I respond.

"Oh, so that means you won?" asks Emily.

Connor chimes in, "Not only did he win, he won big!"

"Really? How big?" asks Emily.

"Oh, it wasn't that much… only a little more than ten thousand dollars," I reply nonchalantly.

"No way!" says Shannon.

"I know. I know. I'm just as astonished as you are," I voice.

"Honey, how did you manage to win ten thousand fucking dollars?" asks Emily.

"It was pretty simple. I didn't do much work. I took fifty bucks and put it on the number eleven at the roulette table. As luck would have it, the ball landed on number eleven. For many of the rolls I decided to sit out, but when I got in on one, I hit. The last roll of the night, I bet big on eleven and it paid off. Before you know it, I had amassed ten grand," I report.

"Emily, I wish you could have seen it. I thought to call you and tell you to come over to the table, but I didn't want to interrupt your fun just to watch me," I tell.

"Alex, it's cool. I'm glad you won. I share in your pleasure even when I'm not with you," replies Emily.

"Enough. Enough. I don't wanna hear that mushy stuff. You can talk like that to each other later on back at the hotel. Please spare me or kill me," says Connor.

"You're just jealous dude, but speaking of the hotel, we need to get back there as soon as possible," I say.

"Why, what's wrong?" asks Shannon.

I tell them that I've already cashed in the chips that I won on the Roulette table. The money's in my pockets and I don't feel comfortable walking around with that much money on me. Somebody could notice I have the money on me and try to harm us. They all agree that the best thing to do is go back to our rooms. It's already three in the morning and we are all quite tired. We have been running nonstop all day.

On the way back to the hotel, we discuss the way I won the money again. The girls are just as excited as the first time I told the story.

"What are your plans for the money?" asks Connor.

"That's a good question. If it's okay with Emily, I'd like to give half to Shannon. I mean it's only right because it was her number that won me the money," I reply.

"I think that's the right thing to do Alex. I have no problem with it," states Emily.

"Dude, I was with you, so does that mean I get a cut too?" asks Connor jokingly.

I don't respond to his silly question, but I do talk to Shannon about how she feels about getting a portion of the money. She is reluctant to accept it because it wasn't her money I was playing with. Eventually, she gives in and agrees to take half of the money. I think she only sided with me to not seem ungrateful.

When we get back to the hotel, I give Shannon her cut of the money. She's not the type of person to carry cash on her, especially in very large amounts. She puts her cut of the winnings in the safe in the room, so she can access it freely. I really have no need to have five thousand dollars cash on me either, so I put some of my winnings in the safe too.

CHAPTER 9

The duration of our trip is filled with much more fun, excitement, and new experiences. We are really living it up. We decide to go to California because it's only a few hours' drive away. None of us have ever been there before, so it's all new to us.

"I'm getting wasted, so I'm not driving. I don't plan on being sober at any point of this trip," I report.

Connor replies, "I totally second that notion. I'm not driving either, so I guess it's on one of you ladies to take the wheel."

"I don't like driving around D.C., so you know there's no way I'm driving in Vegas or California," states Emily.

"Well, I guess that only leaves you Shannon. You're the lucky designated driver. We're relying on you to get us there and back safely. We thank you in advance," I utter.

Shannon replies, "I want to enjoy a few adult beverages just like the rest of you guys. I'm not driving either. I guess we won't be going to California at all. It's not fair that I can't get drunk."

"She's right. We're all here to have a good time and getting drunk is a part of it. We'll just draw straws to see who'll be responsible for us getting to California. We have to go there. We're way too close not to visit," I say.

I grab some straws from the mini bar. We decide the person who draws the longest straw has to take care of getting us there. This game is perfect for where we are. We're in Vegas, so it's only fitting that we gamble a little bit to see who gets the job of driving. I draw the first straw and mine is pretty short, so I think I'm in good shape. The rest of them draw their straws and then we compare them to see who the loser is. As luck would have it, it turns out to be Shannon. We all laugh at her and she's handling it very well. It's like she knows something that we don't.

"Laugh all you want because I'm still not driving. The deal was for the loser to make sure we get there and I will make sure we do just that," Shannon narrates.

"What do you have in mind?" Emily asks.

"I'll either hire a car service or we can take a helicopter. It's only a short flight from Vegas to California," Shannon says.

"The helicopter ride sounds amazing! I would soooo love to do that! Everyone will be jealous when I post the pictures to Facebook and Instagram. We have to do it," responds Emily.

"What do you guys think?" asks Shannon.

"They both sound great to me, but if we take the helicopter ride to California, we'll still need transportation while there. I think the car service is best," I comment.

"I'll be with Jack Daniels the entire time, so it matters to me not. Wherever you say go, I'm going," Connor replies.

"Well, the car service sounds like the best bet, so I'll go online and see what's available. We may be too cramped up in a helicopter anyway," says Shannon.

Shannon makes the arrangements for us to be driven to California. The driver will be here in a couple of hours. We get our overnight bags packed and get ready to go. The ride to the Golden State is awesome. On the way there we stop at the mall that houses the car that the infamous Bonnie and Clyde were in when they were killed. It's a surreal moment for us. With all the bullet holes in the car, it doesn't surprise me that they weren't able to make it out of that gun battle.

The rest of the drive is smooth sailing. We drink, laugh, and blast the music the entire time. Once we arrive in Los Angeles, we immediately go sightseeing. We head to Sunset Boulevard,

Rodeo Drive, and to the Hollywood sign just to name a few. Next, we decide to go to the Beverly Center.

While we're walking around the Beverly Center, my phone rings. I don't want to answer it, but it could be a business call, so I answer it.

"Alex speaking," I utter.

"You fucking pig! My sister was raped and killed herself from the depression she suffered. They never did find the person who raped her, but it was probably you... I'm gonna kill you," voices the caller.

The line goes dead immediately. I tell The Crew about the call I just received. They're upset about the call, but implore me to not let that nonsense ruin our trip. I know I didn't do anything unjust, so my conscience is clear. We resume our fabulous trip.

The shopping in the Beverly Center is great! We see celebrities walking around like it's nothing. The mall has stores in it that we don't have access to back on the east coast. I don't shop a lot, but I've seen so much awesome stuff here that I could go broke. Emily and Shannon are losing their minds in here. They're purchasing everything in sight. They have shoes, purses, scarves, and whatever else you can think of. Connor is just enjoying the moment. He isn't buying anything.

We leave the mall and head to dinner. We're supposed to have dinner reservations, but to no surprise, Connor works around that. The restaurant is very posh and commensurate with Connor's taste. I would have been fine with a burger joint, but that's just me. I'm sure the girls would prefer this place over a burger joint anyway. We really look like celebrities because we have the car outside and we just waltzed right in here. Dinner is fabulous. After dinner, we decide to drive back to Las Vegas instead of spending the night out here. As tired and inebriated as we are, I'm shocked we don't fall asleep on the ride back. Instead, it's just like the ride to California.

We arrive at our hotel at 4 a.m. I take Emily upstairs. When we get to our room, we head straight for the shower. Emily complains of having some slight soreness, so I tell her that I'm going to give her a massage. We kiss and grope one another as we get freshened up. I know this night of drunken sex is going to be epic.

Emily exits the shower, dries off, and leaves the bathroom. A few minutes later I finish showering and walk into the bedroom. Emily is dressed in a sexy lingerie set with a thong on that accentuates her juicy derriere. I tell her to get ready for my magical hands to surf her body.

She rests flat on her stomach as I climb on the bed and kneel behind her. I begin massaging her lower back and continue up her back. I place my hands on her shoulders at the point where her neck and shoulders meet. I notice that she's extremely tense here, so I firmly stroke them to ease the tension. As I maneuver my hands over her body, she moans to signify she's enjoying the treatment. Her sounds remind me of the noises she makes while we're having sex and begin to turn me on. My dick gets harder and harder with every moan she releases.

I pull her thong to the side and push my dick in her slowly. I stroke her pussy sensually and delicately. Her pussy is overwhelmingly wet and hot. I want to enjoy this enchanting feeling for as long as possible, so I pause swimming in her ocean. I rest flat on her back and let my dick sit inside of her, so she can feel its full girth.

"Alex, you have my pussy drenched and my walls stretched so wide," Emily tells in a low sexy tone. "This pussy is all yours!"

As we lie together with our bodies pressed as one. We are in sync with love, passion, and sexual desire. I reach up and pin Emily's hands down and kiss her softly on the back of her neck and earlobes. I lick her along her neck and lightly bite her shoulders. Emily goes wild. I feel a gush of moisture in her pussy like a dam has been breached. My dick still rests inside of her and she's begging for me to resume stroking her, but I don't.

"This is the best pussy I've ever had. No one makes me feel the way you do. I love you Emily," I whisper in her ear as I continue to pin her down.

I want to tease her and enjoy this delightful feeling for as long as possible. Emily takes matters in her own hands. She begins gyrating her body from under me. I feel ever subtle movement she makes. She pushes her body up and then it lowers down. Her ass raises up and then she twists her hips in a circular motion.

"Fuck me," Emily screams.

I let her hands go and wrap one arm around her neck to choke her with. With my free hand I reach under her body and play with her clit. I resume stroking her pussy while I choke her the way she desires. I gently long dick her pussy, so she can feel every inch of my cock. Emily starts screaming and quivering intensely as she cums on my dick, but I don't stop stroking her. She wants to run from the dick, but she can't because I have her locked in. I begin ponding my dick in her pussy with the force that a boxer hit a punching bag. I grunt manly and loudly as Emily wheezes and whiffs with every thrust I give her. Seconds later she begins to tremor again as she cums.

I release her from my clutch and stand up. Emily lies limply on the bed. I'm sure the multiple orgasms have sapped her of most of her energy. However, I'm a raging bull and am still full of vigor. I motion Emily to get up and she complies. We stand at the foot of the bed sharing a tender kiss while she strokes my dick. I drop down to my knees and taste her sweet pussy. Her juices are streaming down her thighs and covering my face. She rubs her hands through my hair as she slowly humps my face while I grip her ass.

I get up off of my knees and suck Emily's succulent titties. I grab her left leg and wrap it around me. I grab my dick and guide it into her pussy as she stands before me. I penetrate her walls tenderly. I quickly switch from short jabs to thunderous thrusts because I'm about to nut. I grip Emily's ass with both hands. I pull her towards my body while I continue poking her forcefully with my dick. The sound of skin smacking infiltrates the air. Emily's screaming and her pussy is farting. The scent of sex permeates the room like a burning candle does.

"I'm about to nut," I yell aloud.

I yank my dick out of Emily and tell her to suck my balls. Emily drops down and licks my balls to my liking. She takes my dick and puts in her mouth. Seconds later the nut is rising up. I pull my dick out of Emily's mouth and nut all over her face and fall to the bed.

Connor and Shannon enjoyed the same type of night as Emily and I did, but they finished long before we did. We have bordering rooms and I could hear their bed banging against the wall. They had a no holds barred fuck fest for sure. At one point, I thought they were trying to compete with Emily and I. If they were, they lost miserably. Emily and I entertain the idea of a second sex session, but we decide to go to sleep instead because we are leaving later this afternoon.

We wake up after what feels like a twenty minute nap and begin packing our bags. The Crew is all showered up and ready to depart from our getaway. I'm actually not excited about leaving because the time was so enjoyable, but we have to get back to reality. Since Connor loaded the car when we left D.C., I volunteer to pack the car up this time.

The girls have a lot more luggage than when we picked them up from the airport the other day. They think it's funny watching me take their stuff down to the car. I shouldn't have chosen to load the car. What was I thinking? Finally, I get the car loaded up and we depart the hotel. We're all starving, so we head to a breakfast place that the locals patronize. We're greeted warmly and seated promptly.

The Crew is pleasantly surprised that the place is immaculate because local businesses have a negative stigma as being unclean and unprofessional. As we sit here, none of us are talking because we're all a little bushed from the long night we just had. I decide to liven up the mood.

"Connor, it sounds like you got some action last night! No blue balls for you," I suggest.

Connor replies, "Well, I am who I am. I've been known to put the slong in all the right places. It's just who I am bud."

We all laugh and the conversation is light and

jovial. I shoot Connor another joke about his sexual performance.

I joke harshly, "You may put your slong in all the right places, but it's not for very long. Sounds like you were doing a quickie stickie."

"No way bro. I'm long and strong. There's no denying it," Connor replies.

"I just know that Emily and I started before you guys and finished well after you two did. I get it. I get it. Maybe you were tired," I remark.

I'm glad Emily is in the restroom because she wouldn't hear of me talking about our sex life in front of other people. She'd wring my neck for sure. Shannon doesn't let me bad talk Connor for very long. She eventually jumps in and defends her man.

"I can testify that he is nothing short of a sexual God. I'm more than satisfied and there are absolutely no shortcomings in regards to stamina or length," Shannon comments.

"Don't make me throw up. I don't wanna hear that garbage. Shannon, you're gonna ruin my appetite," I say jokingly.

"Well, there you have it! I'm a stallion in the bedroom. In fact, you probably could learn a thing or two from me. Pay attention to the master, buddy boy," replies Connor as he pounds his chest.

I say quickly, "I'll pass. I hold my own and very well I might add."

I want to keep the conversation going, but

RYAN HODGE

Emily makes her way back over to us, so I end it. We sit and discuss the events of the trip as well as how much we dread going back to D.C. We love living in D.C., but going back to work is what we aren't looking forward to. I guess this vacation will help us push through until the next trip. We finish eating breakfast and take the ladies to the airport.

As we take their luggage out of the car, Shannon asks, "When are you getting your car from the shop?"

Connor answers, "Alex and I are heading to the shop as soon as we pull away from here. It was only an oil change and tire rotation that I had performed."

We part ways with the girls and we're back on our way to D.C. in no time. A few hours later, I get a text from Emily stating that they landed safely back in D.C. Shannon and Emily had direct flights back to D.C., so they returned home in no time. Unfortunately, Emily said they experienced a good deal of turbulence on the return flight.

According to Emily, they were both nervous and stressed out the entire flight. I'm just glad they landed safely. They'll be over the turbulent flight in no time.

Connor and I finally make it back to D.C. The trip back was without any trouble just like the trip there. I know I'm dreading the work that's before me. I'm sure the rest of this week will be filled with tons of catch up work. That's the only thing about vacations I don't like. There are piles of work when you return.

CHAPTER 10

Fortunately, the work week for Shannon and I wasn't even close to what we imagined it would be. We thought our week would be filled with a tremendous workload because we were gone for several days. However, the week was the exact opposite for us. We essentially were given a full week off. Shannon's company gave her the entire week off because of the hard work she's been doing. Shannon didn't complain one bit because she gets paid time off, but that's not my situation. She doesn't pay me if I don't work. I spent a lot of money in Vegas, so I need to recoup that money. I'm not complaining too much because I did win a few thousand dollars while in there. I guess I'll be using that money to keep from spending money in the bank.

With no work all week, the days were very relaxing and Friday is already here. Shannon,

Connor, Emily, and I have a fun day ahead of us. I'm all rested up and ready to enjoy it. We're staying local today, but we'll have a great time regardless. Connor and I sent a few text messages back and forth and he stated he'll be caught up with business and won't be able to join us until later this evening. Emily is working during the normal business hours for today. Shannon and I don't allow them being tied up to slow us down. We decide to get our day started early. We'll link up with Emily and Connor later.

Shannon picks me up and we head to breakfast at the Breakfast Nook. The service and food is always splendid, so we make it our business to come here whenever possible. I don't think there's another breakfast restaurant in D.C. that comes close to what they offer here. We pull up to the Breakfast Nook and walk in. We are greeted by the host and after a few minutes delay, we're seated.

"I'm not going to lie; I could go for another week off. This is the life," Shannon marvels.

"I agree. It's not all bad. Having nothing to do has its perks, but it also has its disadvantages. I'm not getting paid, but my bills are still coming. You're in a different league than me," I assert.

"I know what I pay you and you're not doing so badly. On top of that, you don't have to pay taxes. Alex, you should be in great shape financially," Shannon claims.

I vocalize, "So you say. I need all the money I

can make. I have a few dollars saved up, but I could always have more. Don't forget that I'm paying rent on two places. Hell, after you deduct the rent for the house you're renting for me and then I pay the rent for my apartment, there isn't much left."

"Yeah. Yeah. We all have bills, so stop crying. Besides, you choose to pay for two residences. Just let the apartment go," Shannon utters.

"I plan to let it go soon, but I'm just not ready yet," I convey.

Shannon states, "Like I said, it's your choice, so don't complain about money when you're clearly wasting it."

I've already explained to her that if I officially move, then I'll have to register as a sex offender in my new neighborhood and I don't want to do that. That was the reason Shannon got me the house in the first place. People deserve to feel safe when they're home and I'm no different. I don't want to be under a constant threat every time I open my front door. Shit, I've been attacked once and that was one too many times.

We enjoy our breakfast and more conversation. I need to go to my official apartment to get my mail and to make sure the place hasn't been vandalized, so we leave the Breakfast Nook and drive over to my place. Shannon and I pull up to my place and walk inside. As we reach the top of steps in the hallway, a guy appears at the bottom of the staircase. We have no idea who he is because his face is covered.

Given my history here, we speed away in the direction of my door. I assume he doesn't have good intentions for us. As we zoom towards my apartment door, the guy flashes a knife and begins to run up the stairs in pursuit of us. Shannon lets out a loud scream as she runs in horror.

"Don't run! I'm gonna gut you like a fish then leave your body to rot like road kill," the unknown assailant screams.

We run up the next flight of stairs with the knife toting predator chasing us. Shannon is terrified and I'm a bit frightened too. I don't know how this is going to end, but I surely don't want to die in the hallway today. There's no prestige in perishing in a hallway. I'll just have to fight for our lives.

I have my keys in hand, so I can insert the key into the door as soon as we get to it. We may have just enough time to get inside my apartment before he makes it to us. While running through the halls, I grab a fire extinguisher and throw it at the guy as he comes up the stairs. Fortunately, it hits him and causes him to stumble backwards. I pass Shannon the keys, so she can open the door just in case I have to fend the man off.

The knife wielding foe regains his composure and keeps coming for us. We get to the door with plenty of time to get inside before he makes it to us, but Shannon does the unforgivable. She drops the keys to the floor because she was shaking uncontrollably from being scared. I swiftly reach down and grab the keys. Unfortunately, the guy moves faster than I hoped he would and is only feet from us as I'm bent over picking up the keys.

Shannon screams, "Oh my God. Watch out Alex!"

The guy raises his hand to swipe the knife at me while I'm bent over. I brace my hands on the floor and without standing up, I horse kick the guy in the stomach and he sails backwards. I grab the keys, stand up, and open the door. Next, I pull Shannon in my apartment and attempt to close the door. Damn, the guy has his foot in the door, so I can't close it all the way. I try with all my might to move his foot, but I can't.

I tell Shannon to get something to hit his foot with to force him to move it. She runs to the kitchen and grabs a pot I have. I try to punch him, but he swipes his knife at me. Fortunately, he misses with the knife and doesn't cut me. She starts banging on his foot with the pot and he immediately pulls it from out the door. I close the door fully and lock it behind me.

"Shannon, call the cops, now!" I order.

Shannon replies, "I left my phone in the car because I thought we'd be in and out."

"Damn, I did the same thing too! I hope the neighbors heard something and they'll call the cops for us," I say.

"Maybe the guy will realize that he can't get us and he'll leave us alone," Shannon states optimistically.

Things get quiet when the guy stops banging on the door. He has to be gone by now unless he's crazy. He wouldn't be dumb enough to risk being in the hallway for an extended period of time squatting on us. Since we don't know for sure, we decide to wait it out. Shannon is scared out of her mind and I'm ready to take action when ready.

I look through my peephole to see if I can see him in the hallway. Unfortunately, I can't see anyone or anything out there. I tell Shannon that I don't see him out there and we agree that he left. I breathe easy because I know we dodged a bullet. Death was really at my doorstep!

I order, "Shannon, let's go! We gotta get out of here now!"

As she scurries for the door, we hear a loud crashing break the silence of the apartment. To our horror, it's a cinder block flying through the window that caused the crashing sound. We look at the window and see the same person who tried to attack us in the hallway climbing through the broken window from the fire escape.

I attempt to unlock the door, so we can exit, but the guy picks up the cinder block and hurls it in our direction at the door. We run from the door and the guy chases us. I put Shannon behind me as the intruder pins us in the corner. I'm going to go out fighting if I have to.

"I'm gonna slit your throat from ear to ear! Your fucking head is gonna be damn near cut off," he states in a low evil whisper.

Shannon begins to tremor with fear. I ball my fists up and prepare to battle for our lives. I move away from Shannon to keep her from inadvertently being injured during our scuffle.

"Man, I know you don't like me for whatever reason, but you don't have to take it out on her. Please, let her go free," I beg.

The guy shakes his head indicating 'no' slowly and swipes the knife at me, but I jump back and he misses me. He takes another swing at me and nearly cuts me. I have to take control of this fight because he'll eventually stab me. It's only a matter of time before my luck runs out. I decide to run to the kitchen and grab a bar stool. I can defend myself better with the stool and may even be able to land a blow to take him down.

He swipes at me again, but misses. Next, I attempt to hit him with the bar stool. While we engage each other, Shannon runs for the door. As she's running for the door, someone starts banging on the door. The guy starts running to stop Shannon from getting to the door, but when he hears someone knocking, he runs in the other direction.

The guy zips out of the window he initially came through. Shannon opens the door and

Connor is standing there. Shannon falls into Connor's arms and weeps uncontrollably. We're glad to see him because he may have just saved our lives. He has no idea what is going on.

"What the hell is going on? Why are you crying?" Connor inquires urgently.

He walks through the door with Shannon draped over him. He sees the broken window and really desires to know what the dilemma is. I begin to tell him what happened to us from the very beginning. He's floored by the details and the horror of our story. He's upset that he wasn't here sooner to stop the guy before he made it inside the apartment.

"Connor, I'm just glad you made it here when you did. Hell, you're the last person I expected to see at the door. I thought you were going to be tied up until we got together later in the evening," I voice.

"Yeah, I was going to be, but one of my appointments canceled on me, so I had some free time. I called you and Shannon to see where you guys were, so I could meet you," Connor explains. "I know when we texted earlier, you mentioned that you had to stop by here, so I figured I'd just drive by to see."

"Honey, I'm sorry. I didn't get the call. I left my phone in the car. We were only running in for a pit stop, so I didn't think to bring it in with me," Shannon reports apologetically.

"Same here. My phone's in the car too. I had

a slow moment and left it on the car charger," I remark.

"No need for apologies, but what we need to do is call the police," Connor states.

He pulls out his phone and is about to dial 911, but I stop him. I explain to them that I don't want the cops here picking through everything. Furthermore, my parole officer will probably assume that I had something to do with this situation and I'm not putting myself in jeopardy of getting violated and being put back in prison.

"I'm just going to fix the window and move forward. I don't know how my parole officer may react to all of this," I verbalize.

"I see where you're coming from, but that guy may come back to hurt you again," Shannon offers.

"You're right about that, but Alex calling the cops won't necessarily keep the perpetrator from coming back in the future," Connor comments frankly.

I reply, "That's my thought precisely! He could just wait until things die down and strike again. I'll never know when he's going to come for me again. Chances are, the police won't be anywhere around to stop him. Shucks, the police won't care about a convicted rapist anyway."

"Okay, I get it. You'll be going through all of the police interaction and police reports for potentially nothing," Shannon vocalizes.

Connor and I begin to cover the window with a sheet and some tape. This makeshift window cover will just have to work for now. We finish with the window and Shannon finally calms down. We decide to not let today's events completely kill our day, so we opt to go get some therapy. Shannon claims she needs a massage to help relieve her tension. She calls a spa to see if they have any available slots. Fortunately, they do, so we drive over.

I decide not to get a massage, so I just hang out in the car. Shannon treats herself to a massage, a manicure and a pedicure. While, I'm waiting in the car, I text Emily to see how her workday is going. She responds to my text and informs me that she's jealous of us today. She would rather be at the spa with us than be at work. We're all going to hang out later today, so I tell Emily not to sweat it.

Finally, Shannon and Connor are done and we leave the spa. Shannon wants to get an outfit for dinner tonight, so she suggests going to the mall. I'm reluctant to go with her because I know this will be no quick endeavor. Connor doesn't go with us because he claims that he has to meet with another client. I don't blame him for dipping out under false pretenses if that's the case. Honestly, I only go because I don't have anything else to do. We spend hours going in and out of every female clothing store in the mall. Shannon eventually makes a purchase from the very first store we went in. Why am I not surprised? I've seen Emily do this exact same thing countless times.

By the time we leave the mall, Connor and Emily are both free. We're meeting up for cocktails and dinner. Shannon drops me home, so I can get dressed for dinner and she goes home for the same reason. Emily, Shannon, and Connor all arrive at my place at 6 p.m. sharp. We all jump into the Mercedes that Connor got for Shannon because we want to ride in style tonight. We arrive at Dee's Winery for cocktails. Dee's is known for having the best vintage wine cellar in our nation's capital. My palate is looking for something other than the everyday drinks. I had enough of the ordinary drinks in Vegas.

We taste many great wines and have many laughs. We also bring Emily up to speed on what happened at my place earlier. She's beyond angered by what we tell her, but she's also very thankful that we're okay. In her opinion, we should've filed a police report. We leave Dee's and drive straight to the restaurant for dinner. The restaurant is impeccable and commensurate to Connor's standards. We really don't need any more wine, but we still enjoy a nice bottle with dinner. The grilled salmon is delicious. In my opinion, this is the best grilled salmon that I've ever had. The rest of our party is in favor of the restaurant too.

We leave the restaurant and go play miniature

golf. We're all tipsy and that makes miniature golf even that much more fun. I'm no good at miniature golf, so being tipsy is my scapegoat for sucking so badly. Surprisingly, Emily is doing better than all of us. I'm surprised because she had just as much to drink as each one of us. After miniature golf, we head back to my place.

"What's next on our agenda?" asks Emily in an excited tone.

Connor replies, "I have no idea what's next on the things to do list. Alex is in control of the next event. I'm just as clueless as you."

"So Alex, spill the beans. We want to know now," says Shannon.

"Don't bite my head off. Geez. What I have in store for us is in that box over there on the counter," I reply.

I retrieve the box off the counter in the living room. I take my sweet time on purpose because I know they're full of anticipation. They're extremely eager to know what's in store. I pull open one flap of the box.

Shannon voices, "I know you don't have a box with board games in it. That's not my idea of how to spend a Friday night D.C. We might as well go to sleep."

Emily replies, "Yeah honey, I have to agree with Shannon. I hope those aren't board games in there. That would be a mood kill for real."

Connor states, "Now, I have known my best bud Alex for a very long time and I stake my reputation on the fact that there aren't any games for us to play in that box."

I comment, "Thanks for having my back on this."

"No prob, but just know that if there are games in that box, I'm gonna have to kill you," voices Connor jokingly.

We all laugh as I assure them that my surprise is much better than board games. I open the remaining flaps of the box and pull out one of the contents of the box. The item is a mask.

"Can anybody guess what I have in mind?" I ask.

"Alex, I had no idea times were so hard for you. We are all friends here. I would give you a loan if you need money, but this is taking things a little too far, don't you think? I'm not into robbing convenience stores. That's illegal for God sakes," says Shannon.

I put my head down and just take the joke. I left myself open for that. Emily laughs hysterically at Shannon's joke. I even join in too.

Connor states, "Everybody put your hands in the air. Nobody has to get hurt. Just do as you're told and you'll be home with your loved ones before long."

He carries the joke further and further. It's all in good spirit. I throw the mask at Shannon to get her to stop laughing. The next thing I pull out of the box is a costume. When the box is empty we all have our own costumes. I purchased the costumes because we are going to the Halloween party at In the Mix tonight.

Emily verbalizes, "I love costume parties!"

"Yeah, me too honey. They allow you to be someone else for the night," I remark.

Shannon says, "They're always a lot of fun. I'm so glad you didn't have board games in the box."

Connor retorts, "I second that. Board games would be spelled B-O-R-E-D."

Everybody tries on their costumes to make sure they fit properly. Shannon and Emily love their costumes. They love the way they fit even more than the costumes themselves. I previously snuck a peek at their sizes to ensure I got costumes that fit them appropriately. Emily is dressed as Tinker Bell and Shannon is dressed as Wonder Woman. Between the two of them, there are more curves in here than a race car track.

Connor has a collection of old Batman comics. He currently has a man crush on him. He won't admit it, but I know he's stoked over the Batman costume I bought him. He now has an excuse to relive his old childhood memories without being made fun of. I'm going to the party dressed as Superman. He was one of my favorite cartoon characters growing up. Connor and I argued all the time about who was the best super hero of all times. He was an adamant supporter of Batman, while I championed Superman to the fullest.

We're all excited about the party, but I think we're more excited about dressing up as characters that we idolized as kids. I'm proud to admit that I'm still a kid at heart. Superman is and will always be my number one.

"Hey bro, remember how we used to get all bent outta shape during our arguments over who's the best super hero of all time?" I ask.

Connor replies, "No way I'd ever forget those. Not even for a sec dude. I remember one time we argued so hard that I left your house and vowed never to talk to you again."

I announce, "I remember that. You tried not to be my friend, but I wouldn't hear of it. I came by every day for a week and forced you into still being my friend."

"I'm so glad you pestered me into staying friends. I couldn't imagine living life without my best bud," confirms Connor. "For the record, Batman is still the best though."

The party is fantastic. The costumes are pretty creative to say the least. In the Mix is filled with just about any character you can think of. The Ninja Turtles, James Bond, and Tina Turner are just a few costumes that are being worn. The DJ pauses the music and Sage announces that Shannon won a gift card as a door prize. I bought Emily one drink too many because she's stumbling all over the place. Shannon is done partying for the night. She's tired and more wasted than Emily and wants to go home, so she can rest. Shannon ridiculously volunteers to drive Emily home while Connor and I stay behind. Connor and I decide the night is over and it's time to leave.

"Alright party poopers, I guess it's time we go, but I have to drain the main vein first," I say.

Connor jumps in, "I have to hit the latrine too. Let's go bro."

We go to the bathroom and then return to the booth we left Emily and Shannon at. We say goodbye to a few people and head to the car. My three amigos aren't in the best of shape, so getting to the car is quite comical. They all stagger to the car, but they make it without falling down.

"You may be in a costume as Superman, but it doesn't hide the fact that you're a fucking rapist," someone utters as I attempt to close the door behind myself as I sit in driver's seat.

I'm horrified because I recognize that voice as being the voice of the person who attacked me at my apartment. I'm pulling the door with all of my might, but I can't close it because the guy is pulling it in the opposite direction. He's swinging a knife at through the small opening of the door. Emily and Shannon are screaming at the top of their lungs. Shannon is nudging Connor, but he's sleep in a drunken stupor.

Emily voices, "I'm gonna go get help!"

Emily and Shannon bolt from the car to find help. Shannon calls 9-1-1 as they run away. The man is yanking the door over and over again and makes my hand slip off the door. When the door shakes free of my hand, the perpetrator comes running toward me. I know I have to fight him, so I kick him and stand up.

"I'm your kryptonite, Superman. You're gonna bleed like Superman never has," the man speaks as he swipes at me.

Shannon and Emily haven't returned, and Connor is still unconscious.

His first swipe misses me, but I punch him in the face. He stumbles back from the impact of the blow. I'm scared shitless, but I have to defend myself. He fakes like he's going to stab at me again, so I jump back to avoid the impact. Unfortunately, his fake attempt to stab me was a setup for the real attempt. He slices my arm clean and breaks the skin. Blood is streaming down my arm.

He tries the same maneuver again, but this time I'm ready. I grab his hand the he's holding the knife with and we tussle. I raise his arm over his head and knee him in the ribs. The knife falls to the ground. Next, he clips my leg from under me and I fall to the ground.

Sadly, I can't reach the knife. The guy mounts me and is pins my arms down with his knees. To my horror, he reaches over and grabs the knife off the ground. He raises the knife over his head and swoops it down to stab me with it. I'm able to get one hand free to block his attempt, but he's still pressing the knife towards my throat.

My arm is quite tired and the knife is inching closer and closer to my neck. My mind is saying keep fighting, but my body is fatigued and is not cooperating. I know this isn't going to end well, but I'm still pushing him with all my might. I feel the blade beginning to pierce my neck. It's a slight pinching sensation and it's only a matter of time before it goes all the way through.

I close my eyes because I don't want to see it coming. I feel like I'm watching myself die and it's terrifying. With my eyes closed, I feel the man's weight quickly lift off of me. Connor finally woke up and pushed the guy off of me. Connor in his drunken state didn't deliver a debilitating blow to the man because he runs off as soon as Connor hits him.

"Dude, are you alright? Connor questions.

"I'm fine thanks to you! I thought I was a goner bro. You saved my life!" I report.

"You would have done the same for me. I'm just glad you're alive. That was a close call," Connor offers.

Emily and Shannon return with some security guards who were inside. Emily's all shaken up even though the danger is over. She's freaking out over the blood that's on my arm even though it's nothing serious. Moments later Sage comes out to investigate. The cops and ambulance arrive shortly thereafter. The police take statements from all of us about the incident while the emergency worker patches me up. After a long night, we all head back to my place.

During the drive home, Connor, Emily, and Shannon still all manage to fall asleep. I'm in good shape because I haven't had much to drink and the scuffle has my blood pumping. We arrive at my place safe and sound. I had a ball tonight even with the unexpected drama.

I pull into the garage and wake Connor up first. He jumps out of the car and runs straight to the bathroom because he's about to throw up. I guess I have to get the girls out of the car myself. Next, I wake Emily up and help her to my bedroom. She leans on me all the way upstairs.

"I'll be back with a late night dessert for you soon. I hope you're ready," I comment sexually.

I go back downstairs and pull Shannon out of the car and walk her upstairs. She's in and out of consciousness. I call out to Connor for help, but he isn't responding. Getting Shannon upstairs would be a lot easier if Connor was able to help. Oh well, I have to do what I have to do. I finally get Shannon to the room after struggling mightily. I run back downstairs to check on Connor. He's now on the couch in a deep slumber. I decide not to try to carry him upstairs. I know my limitations.

Upstairs I go and enter the room. The room is pitch-black when I enter. I would normally turn the light on, but I don't want to ruin the mood. Besides, tonight's different and I'm in a real freaky mood. Tonight, I'm a thief in the night. I'm not me tonight because I'm role playing.

I navigate through the room in the dark. I just need to find my bed and I'll be fine. I won't need to see with my eyes for what's going to happen in the bed. My tongue will end up in the right destination I'm sure.

Fortunately, I make it to my bed without falling over anything. There's just enough light in the room for me to see the silhouette of my delicious treat resting in bed. I'm so turned on that my dick is getting hard just off the thought of penetrating her walls again.

I kneel down at the foot of the bed to plan my attack. How should I wake her up? Should I snatch the cover off, should I call her name softly until she awakens, or should I use my mouth in a more pleasing way for both of us? I think she'll prefer my mouth in a pleasing way.

I slightly lift up the sheet giving myself just enough room to slither underneath it. I don't want her to feel anything before my lips touch her. I'm under the covers and begin kissing her up her legs. I gently part her legs and smooch her inner thighs. I can tell she's beginning to awaken and realize what's going on.

She spreads her legs wider apart to give me unrestricted access to the treasure that I'm invading for. After licking her inner thigh, I lick her clit and fondle her vaginal area. Her pussy is soaked and I haven't even started fucking her yet.

RYAN HODGE

I feel like teasing her, so I lick her clit then stop
and repeat the same thing over and over. We're
both into it as I keep eating her pussy.

"Ooh," she moans.

I lick a little faster because I want more of a
response. She moans again with more intensity.
I can tell her body is becoming overtaken by
sexual desire. My tongue strokes are causing her
to be filled with pleasure. I stick my tongue
inside her pussy while I rub her clit.

"Yes, right there. Don't move baby that's it!
That's the spot," she says.

Her lower extremities are gyrating to the beat
that my tongue is licking her pussy. We're one
with each other. My face is saturated from her
juices. She has one hand squeezing her breast
and nipple and the other hand is under the cover
stuffing my face into her pussy.

I don't know if I'm going to die from
drowning or suffocation, but I'm not stopping
what I'm doing because I'm caught up in the
moment. I decide to push the envelope tonight.
I lick my pointer finger and reach under her and
start rubbing her asshole. She doesn't stop me
and responds pleasantly.

She says, "Oooh, I like that."

I continue eating her out while I gently caress
her asshole. The assortment of sensations is
driving her crazy. She's no longer grabbing her
breasts and stuffing my face in her pussy.
Instead, she's using her hands to pull herself up

the bed by grabbing the headboard. She's running from pleasure and it turns me on even more. I chase her up the bed without stopping what I'm doing.

"I wanna feel your dick now!" she demands.

She's ready to feel my rod and I'm more than happy to give it to her. All of this foreplay has me ready to blow my load. I hope I can hold it back because I want to enjoy this for as long as I can. I'm really not the least bit interested in a quickie right now.

I pull her down to the foot of the bed and flip her over. I want to fuck her doggy style tonight. I have a lot of steam to get off and fucking her from the back will enable me to do just that. She's ready and waiting for what I'm about to deliver. Her tight plump ass is tooted up right in front of me.

Her pussy is so wet that I can feel the juices down her leg. I insert myself into her pussy. She takes a deep breath and then exhales. Her body tenses up from feeling the full girth of my dick. I don't move my dick or stroke her at all. I savor the moment before I begin to thrust her. I can't get my mind over how wet she is.

I slowly begin to stroke her pussy. As I speed up, her moans become screams. As her moans become screams, my strokes become violent hard bombs. She buries her face in the pillows to keep from waking the others. I continue pounding and then I lick my finger and insert my it into her ass.

As I penetrate her pussy with my dick, I insert my finger in and out of her booty.

I had no idea she would enjoy it this much. She pushes back to receive deeper penetration from both my finger and dick. She pounds the bed in pure euphoria from the treatment her body is receiving. Her pussy is gushing so much that my balls are soaked. I can't hold my load anymore and neither can she.

I feel myself about to bust, so I speed up my strokes. I want to get the most thunderous release I can possibly get. I feel her pussy tighten up around my dick and she starts screaming. At that point, I yank my finger out of her ass to help intensify her orgasm. She's panting as if the orgasm is still going on. While she's moaning, I feel her cheeks smacking back on my dick and I shoot my load all over her ass. My heart is pounding so rapidly that it feels like it's going to jump out of my chest.

She falls flat on her stomach and does not move. She falls into a deep slumber. I guess she needed that more than I did. I hear a loud noise come from the living room, so I head back downstairs. When I get back to the living room, Connor's not on the couch. He's back in the bathroom with his face in the toilet. I hope he's not mad at me for leaving him downstairs by himself. This is what he gets for drinking out of control.

"Dude, are you going to be alright?" I inquire

sincerely.

"Bro, I'm fine. I feel a lot better after throwing up this last time. Sorry, I had to let it go in your place," Connor verbalizes.

I convey, "Man, it's nothing. I'm just glad you made it to the bathroom. Trust me, I've put far worse into that toilet. You haven't scratched the surface with that puke."

"Oh, come on guy. You didn't have to make me visualize that while I have my face in the toilet," Connor shoots back. "You're gonna make me throw up from the thought of you shitting in here."

We both laugh as I help Connor up from the floor. It's late, so we decide to call it a night. The night has been long and eventful and I'm beat. I walk Connor upstairs and then I go to my room and fall out on the bed.

CHAPTER 11

I wake up around 1 p.m. and Emily is still fast asleep. I wonder if Shannon and Connor are awake. I get out the bed and go downstairs to see if they're awake. After a quick check, I notice nobody else is up, so I decide to turn on the television in the living room. Moments later, Emily comes downstairs and joins me.

"Good morning, beautiful," I greet.

"Hi, honey," she replies warmly.

I inquire, "Did you sleep well?"

"Yes, you know I did. I didn't move once you went back downstairs. I was like a person in a coma," Emily speaks.

We both chuckle at the joke. I begin to make breakfast, but Emily doesn't want any. She has many errands to run in preparation for the upcoming work week, so she's leaving.

"Tell Shannon and Connor I'll see them soon.

There's no telling what time they'll wake up. They had a lot more to drink than I did last night, so I'm sure they'll need more time to sleep the alcohol off than I did," Emily voices.

I utter, "I'm sure you're right. They were pretty wasted last night. Text me later when you finish running your errands."

"I will. Make sure you take care of that cut. See you later," she articulates.

I begin to walk Emily to her car, but as I open the door for her, I hear my breakfast sausages sizzling, so I quickly run back to the kitchen because I don't want them to burn. My hustle back to the kitchen to keep them from burning was all for nothing because Shannon is taking them out of the pan.

"A woman's job is never done. Be beautiful, sex a man's brains out, and keep men from burning the house down," Shannon comments comically.

"You forgot to include give birth to the kiddies. And for the record, I had everything under control in here. Nothing to worry about," I declare.

Shannon chimes in, "Right, right. I guess burnt sausages are perfect for breakfast."

"I'll just say that I like my sausages crispy. That's all," I reply.

Out of nowhere, Connor says, "Something sure smells delicious. Breakfast is right on time too because I'm starving. Thanks, for making me breakfast darling. You must have read my mind."

I choose not to tell him that I'm the one who was initially cooking breakfast. All that matters is that the food is being cooked. Connor walks up behind Shannon while she cooks and pokes her with his lower half.

"Come on Connor. I don't want to throw up like you were last night. I don't need to be privy to your sugary sweet activities," I remark.

"You can always close your eyes or leave the room," Connor delivers.

"Last time I checked, this was my place," I declare.

Connor quickly replies, "This is actually Shannon's place if you wanna go by the letter of the lease."

I insist, "Now, that's colder than an iceberg in Antarctica."

The three of us share in a laugh as we eat breakfast. We enjoy light conversation about the day before and continue teasing one another.

I express, "This may not be my place and I'm fine with that, but Shannon, you have to admit that the pump Connor gave you while cooking was a short stroke. It was short just like the ones he gave you in Vegas."

"He's fabulous in that department as I said before. That joke is so overdone. I'm bored with it," Shannon maintains.

"Dude, if I remember correctly, you didn't get your first piece of action until I set you up with

Mary. You blew your load while you were putting the condom on," I contend.

"That was a long time ago buddy boy. I've gotten my stamina up since then and learned many new tricks. I'm almost like a porn star now," Connor asserts.

"Porn star, huh? Have you lost your wits?" I ask.

Shannon comments, "You should listen to him. He has a myriad of sexual tricks up his sleeve. Last night, Connor fucked me like he was the Greek God of sexual desire- Eros. I'm sure you heard my screams of pleasure."

"Thanks Shannon, but you don't have to make up stories for me. I know my skills and endowments," Connor replies.

"Honey, I'm not making up stuff. I wouldn't do that. I'm talking about the great sexual encounter you gave me last night. I was beyond satisfied," Shannon says.

"I understand what you're saying, but we didn't have sex last night. I was out of it. I was bombed," Connor replies.

"You clearly had too much to drink last night because we had sex for sure and I had multiple orgasms. I'm shocked you don't remember," Shannon states. "You were amazing!"

Connor asks, "What the hell are you talking about?"

"You shouldn't drink so much. Look I even have the message you sent stating you were on your way to sex me," Shannon says.

She shows Connor the message and he's clueless as to what she's referring to. He tells her again that he didn't fuck her and that he didn't send the message. I decide to intervene in their conversation.

I say, "You were wasted, so you don't know what was going on dude."

"Yes, you had too much to drink and were wasted. I was in a dreamland while you were handling my sexual desires. That position you had me in had my walls stretched more than normal. It's like you had more girth," Shannon reports.

Connor states, "I could have sworn I was dreaming that we had sex. I mean the dream was extremely vivid, but it just didn't seem like I was awake."

"It's official! No more drinks for you buddy. You can't tell a dream from reality when you're inebriated. This is classic dick head material," I reply as I give him a noogie.

"I know. Maybe I'll slow it down a little bit, but not all that much. I've always loved a good drink and besides it was Halloween! We all know that the freaks come out on Halloween," Connor states.

Shannon shakes her head and we both laugh at Connor. This isn't the first time he's forgotten something he's done after a night of drinking. I can't talk too badly about him because I've done many things while under the influence. Some of those things I regret and some I don't. Honestly, I don't recall a lot of things that happened while I was drunk.

Connor finishes his breakfast and leaves. Shannon stays behind and begins to put the dishes away. She snatches Connor's plate from the table and slams it in the sink. The breaking of the plate gives off a loud smashing sound. Pieces of the broken plate scatter throughout the kitchen. I'm astonished by Shannon's action because it was clearly done on purpose. I rush to the sink to investigate Shannon's dilemma.

I immediately inquire, "What's wrong? Why'd you destroy the plate like that?"

"I'm so fucking livid," Shannon says as she pulls away from me.

She starts cursing and yelling to the point that I can't make out what's she saying. Seconds later tears begin to stream from her eyes.

"Shannon, I have to say you're really freaking me out right now! You have to tell me what's troubling you, so I can help. You're acting real bipolar right now," I speak.

"I don't need your help or anyone else's. I'm fine. Trust me; I'm fine," Shannon asserts as she exits the kitchen.

"So what's your deal then?" I ask as I follow her to the living room.

"My deal? If you really wanna know my fucking deal, I'll tell you. You and Connor, or at a bare minimum you, are really full of shit. I'm not a bumbling idiot even though you may think I am!" Shannon yells angrily.

"Shannon, what the hell are you talking about?" I inquire.

"Don't play dumb with me! You know damn well what I'm talking about!" Shannon screams at the top of her lungs.

"No, I really am clueless. I haven't the slightest idea of what you're screaming for. Enlighten me please," I reply.

"The late night fuck! I know that was you who fucked me last night. You conniving bastard! I can't fucking believe you!" Shannon charges violently.

"I have no idea what you're talking about," I remark.

"Alex, stop the charade. Like I said before, I'm not an airhead. I knew something wasn't quite right when who I thought was Connor had sex with me. It just didn't feel the same as normal," Shannon narrates.

"I don't know what to tell you. All I know is that it wasn't me. I was nowhere near your room," I reply.

"That's bullshit! You know at first I was just gonna dismiss the thought of that not being Connor, but when he didn't recall any of it, I knew my suspicions were right. The person I had sex with wasn't Connor for sure, but magically felt just like you did the night we had sex in the car. I bet you can't explain that," Shannon claims.

"You've lost your mind Shannon. I have done no such thing. You know me better than that. You know I'd never do something like that to you, Connor, or Emily," I declare.

"You don't tell me what I know. I know Connor's hands are much smaller than yours and the hands that caressed my body last night were huge. I know I was drunk, but even the penetration was much deeper inside of me," Shannon states.

Shannon is extremely worked up and is hitting me as I deny the accusations against me. She's still yelling profanities incessantly and crying uncontrollably. Her face looks like she was splashed with a water balloon. She's hitting me so much that I have to pull her arms down to her sides before she hurts me.

She wiggles and squirms to get me off of her. I don't let her free until she promises to stop assaulting me.

"Okay, okay damn it! You're right. It was me last night who you had sex with," I confess.

Shannon cuts me off before I finish and states, "Let's be clear on one thing, we did not have sex. What you did is called rape. Rape by deception to be exact. You'll pay for this dearly and so will Connor if he had anything to do with it!"

I explain to Shannon that I made a bonehead decision to trick her into having sex with me. I also tell her that Connor had nothing to do with my ruse to sleep with her. She wants to know every intricacy of my plan. An abbreviated explanation is not satisfying her appetite for the truth, so I fully disclose everything.

"I thought maybe you wanted to feel me inside of you like you did the night we celebrated passing the bar exam," I convey. "I saw the way you were looking at me all night. You're complicit in this too. You had been flirtatious all night."

"Well, clearly you thought incorrectly. Poor Emily will be distraught and Connor's going to whoop your ass! You better hope this doesn't ruin my relationship with Connor. I finally meet a great guy and you pull this shit. Gee, thanks!" Shannon replies.

"Do you really have to tell them? Can't this be our little secret? Can't we just let it be like they what say about Vegas?" I ask.

"Alex, I'm really disgusted by the sight of you and the sound of your voice right now. I don't care to hear any of your untimely jokes. This is no laughing matter," Shannon reports.

"You act like we haven't had sex before. I know you enjoyed it. You were in heaven," I remark.

My comment doesn't sit well with Shannon. She stops talking while she gathers the rest of her belongings. I don't attempt to try to get her to talk anymore. I know she's at a point of no return. The last thing I want is for her to start hitting me again. Shannon makes it back downstairs after getting her things and walks away.

As Shannon gets into her car she states, "I can't believe that you would state that rape is the victim's fault."

I don't get a chance to respond because she slams the car door behind her. She throws the car in reverse and backs out of the driveway. I really didn't see this situation going this way. I didn't see this much conflict coming from this. In my opinion, it was only one night of fun and we should keep it between us. I guess I can't expect people to see things exactly the same way as I do.

I go upstairs to my room and sprawl across the bed and evaluate my current situation. What is my next move going to be? There are many things to consider now that Shannon is upset with me. I doubt that she'll continue giving me work to do, so I need to consider what I'll do for work when my money runs low.

CHAPTER 12

This is so screwed up. If she's mad enough, she may even put me out of the house she's renting for me. I hope I don't have to go back to bartending at In the Mix. The pay is awful and I'll be back where I started. If she tells Connor, he may be upset with me. I think I need to tell him first, so I can put my slant on the story. He'll understand where I'm coming from. Now Emily on the other hand, she'll be out of my life for sure.

I call Connor and tell him a very different version of what really happened that night in the bedroom. I tell him 'my' entire story and he's all ears. My best bud takes the news well and lets me know that it's okay. He knows how things happen when people get drunk. The conversation never turns to a negative or aggressive tone. Connor and I have been through worse. We always vowed to never let a woman come between us and we're sticking to that pact today. This is why Connor is my best friend. He'll do anything for me and always has my back. We hang up the phone and I relax for a few hours before I fall into a deep sleep.

The next morning I'm awakened by my phone ringing. I'm in such a deep slumber that I initially think the phone ringing is a part of my dream. I soon realize that it is in fact ringing, so I pick my head up from under the covers and look at the phone screen. Surprisingly, it's Shannon calling me. What could she want this early? Why is she calling me after she just was upset with me yesterday?

I say groggily, "Hello."

"You told Connor about what happened before I did and then didn't even tell him the truth. Now, he's mad at me for not telling him what happened immediately. He's livid and feels like I intentionally hid what happened from him. Connor called me and questioned me intensely about what happened that night. Apparently, he feels like I was never gonna tell him and you know that's not the case. You need to talk to him," Shannon explains.

"I guess you should've told him first. That's not my problem. I have enough to think about without having to worry about your relationship woes. You need to handle your own affairs," I say.

"I wasn't gonna tell Emily, but since you wanna act as if I'm on my own, I guess you'll be on your own too. We'll see how Emily takes the news that you cheated on her. I'm sure she'll distance herself from you too," Shannon narrates.

"Ultimately, you're going to do exactly what you want to do anyway, so have at it. Whatever floats your boat. I have myself to consider. I'm done talking," I verbalize.

"Oh no Mister, you aren't done talking yet. You may not talk to me, but I'm sure the police will be interested in talking to you. They'll make you talk to them for sure," Shannon says.

"The police? What do they want with me?" I eagerly reply.

Shannon answers, "Oh, they won't want much. They'll just be bringing you up on charges for rape asshole!"

"As you are very well aware, I've been brought up on bogus rape charges before, so this is nothing new and just more of your bullshit Shannon. To hell with you!" I yell.

"Is that what this is about? You're still caught up in the past? Didn't you say we were going to bury the hatchet and move on?" Shannon inquires.

"This isn't only about the past Shannon. It's about right now and past moments. You curse me out and threaten me, but you want me to remain civil. You falsely accused me of rape in the past and now you threaten me again with the same thing. I don't care anymore, so fuck you," I voice.

I have no patience for her. She wants me at her beck and call after she ruined my life. She wants me to have sympathy for her because she may have lost a boyfriend. Well, I don't. Shannon should have sympathy for me because I lost my freedom and essentially my life.

How dare she approach me with threats of calling the police! Even if it is considered rape now, I'm justified because I'm innocent of the first time she called rape. Let's be for real, she enjoyed every stroke of it. There's no way she couldn't tell who I was or she at least knew it wasn't Connor, but she went along with it.

Shannon replies, "I just want you to know that I'll be contacting your precious Emily and the police before the day's end. See you in court rapist!"

"And I'll see you in court! You're nothing more than a liar and a whore," I respond violently.

"That's funny! I'm a whore, but you went through a tremendous amount of planning to sleep with me. By the way, I'm changing the locks on MY house that I allowed you to stay in, so pack your shit up and get out before your stuff lands in the garbage dump," Shannon orders.

"I have a place to go to, so I'm not worried. I'll gladly leave this place. I'll be out before you know it," I state.

Shannon says, "Oh that's right! You'll go back to the apartment where they almost killed you. Maybe the next time they try they'll be successful."

"Trust me, I'll find something better. You don't worry about me. There's not a worrisome bone in my body or thought in my head," I comment arrogantly.

"If you consider prison better than your apartment, then I'm happy for you because that's where you'll be soon," Shannon replies.

"Fuck off! I won't be in prison again. I guarantee you that. You fool me once - shame on you, fool me twice - shame on me. And by the way, the sex was average at best. I wasn't impressed," I say.

I hang up before Shannon can utter another word. I'm tired of hearing her voice. I only have a few things to pack from the place Shannon rented for me, so my move will be simple. Anything that's here now can. I couldn't just empty my apartment out because my parole officer frequently makes visits. The transition back there will be smooth sailing for me. The house she rented for me is very nice though, but all good things come to an end. Besides, I'm sure I'll get all of that stuff back. I leave the house and head to my apartment.

Unfortunately, two hours later, Connor and Shannon show up to my apartment without telling me they were going to stop by. I hope they aren't planning to stay long because my parole officer (PO) is going to pay me a visit today. I really don't want them to be here when he arrives. I don't want to have to explain who they are or even introduce them to my PO.

I open the door hesitantly and they walk in angrily. My first thought is that they are going to pummel me as soon as they have an opening, but I soon dismiss that idea because Connor would never put his hands on me. I know Shannon's anger is directed towards me, but I don't know why Connor isn't looking me in the eye. Shannon won't look me in the eyes and has not greeted me, which is customary for when we see each other. I know she's livid about us having sex at my place.

"Dude, I never jump to conclusions about things I hear about you, so I'm asking you openly, honestly, and respectfully about something Shannon told me," Connor says.

"Sounds real serious. I'll answer your questions with as much honesty and detail I possibly can," I respond.

"Okay, thanks bro. I appreciate that," Connor replies.

I say, "No problem. Get to your questions. I wanna help ease whatever's on your mind."

"The morning after the Halloween party, Shannon made mention of me and her having sex," says Connor.

"Yeah, I remember that. You were too wasted

to remember. You're a lush dude," I say jokingly.

"That's the thing dude. I know I was drunk, but I wasn't drunk to the point where I wouldn't remember a sexual encounter," Connor speaks.

"I understand. I wouldn't forget that either. Especially, if it was real good," I comment.

"I'm trying to figure out when I was able to have sex with her. Actually, I'm saying that I didn't have sex with her. Shannon told me that the sexual encounter took place after we got back from the party," Connor states.

"Okay, you two had a late night tryst. I don't see where this is going," I say.

"Well, around that time is when I was throwing up in the bathroom downstairs. Then you left me sleeping on the couch," Connor reports.

"What are you getting at? Are you implying that I had sex with Shannon bro?" I ask.

"No, you bastard! It wasn't sex; it was rape!" Shannon screams.

"Now that's way off base. I didn't rape you. Don't say that," I reply.

Connor states, "I'm not implying anything that's why I'm asking you what you know about that night, but I'll be honest it doesn't look good on your part. All you said on the phone was that you slept with her and rubbed on her before realizing you weren't in your own bedroom. And Shannon told me you admitted it outright that you two had sex."

The longer Connor thinks about what happened, the more agitated he gets. I can tell that he wants answers. He looks like Bill Bixby slowly turning into the incredible hulk.

"Alright, I texted Shannon from your phone after I left you in the bathroom. I went upstairs to your room and I did have sex with Shannon," I confess.

Shannon yells, "You're a pig! You're an animal and I hate you for that. I could kill you!"

Shannon begins to cry profusely. Connor embraces her as he gives me the stare of death. He looks at me as if I've stolen his heart. All I can think is that they need to leave before my parole officer arrives. If my parole officer comes here and hears this, he will violate me for sure and send me back to prison. I'm really not looking to have that happen.

"I thought we were better friends than this man. You slept with my lady. I would have never guessed this in a million years," Connor remarks angrily.

"Come on bro. It's not that serious. You two are overreacting. Besides, Shannon wanted it. She was begging for the goods. I just made it easy for her and let her off the hook. I could tell that she enjoyed every minute and every stroke," I shoot back.

"You know what? Fuck you Alex!" Shannon says as she attempts to break free from Connor's grip to put her hands on me.

Connor states, "Dude, this is so not cool. This is really low. This is a total violation that I can't even put into words. You're a fucking joke. A real douche."

"Come on bro. You know it's not that serious. We've shared our girls in the past. I don't see what's different now," I tell.

"Exactly! In the past! That stuff was years ago in college. We're years beyond that. Besides that, Shannon is different. I love her and she loves me. You have to understand that we're a couple. This is not just for kicks," Connor dictates.

"Connor, trust me. I'm telling you that she wanted it. She wanted it badly. If she didn't, she wouldn't have had such massive orgasms."

"Asshole, we're blowing out of here," Connor announces in an irritated fashion.

"You liked it, didn't you Shannon? It felt good, didn't it Shannon?" I ask.

Shannon buries her head in Connor's chest as she cries some more. I don't know if she's crying from guilt because she really enjoyed it or because she's really angry. Whatever the reason is, Connor is clearly upset by Shannon's emotional state.

"I'm sorry honey. I'll take care of this. He can't hurt you like this," Connor says to Shannon. Connor pulls Shannon's head from his chest and looks her in the eye. Next, he wipes her tears away. After he wipes her tears away, he lunges toward me. I'm caught totally off guard by his quick move and I pay the price for it. Connor slams me down to the floor with nearly no resistance from me.

Unfortunately, the crushing blow to the floor knocked the wind out of me. I'm unable to fully fight back after that. Connor grabs me around my neck and chokes even more of my breath out of me. I feel myself going out of consciousness. Connor stops choking me just before I pass out. Next, he punches me in the ribs several times.

Things get so out of hand that Shannon even gets in a couple of hits on me. I guess she feels like she's entitled to a few blows. Eventually, Connor is satisfied with the physical assault he's given me because he stops and gets off of me.

"You're a loser. You're not even worth an ass whooping," Connor comments.

"I hope you don't think because you got your ass whooped that this is over for you. I want you to know that this is merely the beginning of the end for you," remarks Shannon.

My ribs hurt and I'm out of breath. I don't even have the energy to respond to her warning or threat. I just want them to leave. I need to straighten the place up before my parole visit. Talk about poor timing. Connor storms out of my apartment. Shannon attempts to grab him to stop him, but he yanks his arm away from her and leaves her behind. Shannon grabs her purse and storms out after him.

My parole officer shows up just as I finish

straightening up. He talks to me for about thirty minutes and then he leaves. I'm fortunate that he didn't notice anything awry. He praises me for maintaining a clean criminal record during my time on parole.

A few hours later, my phone rings. It's Emily and she's crying. She's crying, blowing her nose, and trying to talk all at the same time. Her words are unintelligible. I have no idea what she's saying, but I'm sure I could guess. I'd bet money that she talked to Shannon and is abreast of the situation. I'm really not in the mood to talk to Emily right now.

She's emotional and I'm not, so the conversation really can only go one way. Her feelings will be hurt and I won't care. I'll talk to her tomorrow or the day after when I have the patience and understanding to indulge her. I hang up the phone purposely. I'm sure she knows it wasn't accidental, but I don't care. After I hang up on her, I sprawl across my bed.

Twenty minutes later, there's a ferocious banging on my door. I'm sure from the intensity of the knocking that it's the police coming to take me into custody. I put on some comfortable pants and tennis shoes and head to open the door. To my surprise, it's not the cops at the door, it's Emily. I guess since she couldn't reach me on the phone after I hung up on her, she felt the need to come over.

I open the door and she comes in crying. I

disinterestedly ask her why she's crying and she tells me the news she got from Shannon. I assure her that all is well and I didn't sleep with Shannon. There's no need to have Emily's feelings hurt because of Shannon and her selfish ways. This is one of those times when telling a lie is beneficial not only to me, but also to the person the lie is being told to.

Emily asks a million questions as to why Shannon would make up such an unimaginable story. I draw conclusions for her to help ease her mind. Next, I cue up a recording and let Emily listen to some of it and she's eventually at ease. She apologizes for taking Shannon at her word before talking to me first. Emily leaves totally opposite from the way she arrived.

She's happy and relieved that I didn't cheat on her and is fully supportive of me now. I'm glad that's taken care of because it's just one less thing to worry about. I spend the rest of the day wondering when the police would call me. Fortunately, they never do. I love cops when they're not trying to question me, but I don't like them when I'm on the wrong side of the law. This will be my last dealings with the law from the standpoint of a suspect.

I have a few drinks after Emily leaves and fall asleep into a drunken stupor. I sleep well into the next day, awaking at 3 p.m. I have another thunderous knock at the door, but this time, it is the police. The cops want me to go down to the station with them to answer a few questions. I comply with their request and we head to the station.

When I get to the interrogation room, the D.C. police inform me that Shannon alleges that I raped her on Sunday morning. Since the alleged crime took place in their jurisdiction, they want to ask me some questions. I answer their questions to the best of my ability. I deny all accusations about raping Shannon. I tell them that I can't offer much insight because I don't know anything.

I offer up whatever information I can to the detectives. The detectives are very interested in the other information I have in the case, so they want to talk to me again very soon. They're kind enough not to take me into custody and instead let me leave, but tell me not to leave the area. I'd much rather travel freely on my own accord than to be arrested. I make my way back to the station later that same day.

"Thanks for coming back so soon Mr. Huggins. I'm Detective Brian Lewis. I wasn't sure you would make it back. We took a bet here at the station to see if you'd make it or not. I lost 20 bucks because of you," the detective says jokingly.

"No, thank you for allowing me to come back to the station at my own will. I really appreciate that. Call me Alex please. I didn't mind coming back because I want more than anything to clear my name," I vocalize.

"Well, Alex, you'll have an opportunity to do so today. Follow me to the interrogation room. It's this way," orders the detective.

I talk to the detectives and tell them my side of the story and tell them the history that exists between Shannon and me. They're floored by the information I put before them. They decide not to bring charges on me at this time, but inform me that the investigation is ongoing. I'm very pleased by that because it's a step in the right direction. I know they have to complete things on their end of the investigation. They inform me that they want to talk to all parties involved. It's all a part of the process to find out the truth and to see this thing all the way through.

The police are able to get in contact with Emily before Connor. They tell Emily to come to the station just as they had me report to the station. Fortunately, she isn't going have a police escort like I initially did. She's a little traumatized by the whole interrogation process, but she handles it very well. Everything goes accordingly.

No one has been able to contact Connor to get his side of the story. His phone is disconnected. Shannon, against my liking, keeps calling me to see if I've heard something from him. She feels like he turned his phone off to keep from having to deal with her and blames me for it. If she keeps calling and texting me, I'm going to change my number.

How is she calling me for help when she claims I raped her again? This is beyond my level of understanding. I've told her on many instances to stop calling me, but she persists. I wonder if I can get a restraining order on a person who has accused me of rape. I don't know for sure, but I'm going to look into it.

Two days later, Connor finally resurfaces from his impromptu hiatus. It's only been days, but it seems like weeks. I guess with all that's going on with this investigation it just makes time drag by. Someone is calling me from a number a number that's not stored in my phone. I contemplate not answering the call because I don't know who it might be. I decide to answer it because it might be Connor and it turns out it is him.

"Well, Connor's back from the dead. It's about time I'm hearing from you," I say jokingly.

"Right, Connor's dead alright. This is my new number. I can be reached here. I went back home to Jersey for a few days. Had some things to handle there, but I'm back in town now," Connor reports.

"Well, I'm glad you're back because the police need to interview you," I inform.

Connor asks, "The cops wanna interview me regarding what?"

"Well, Shannon has gone to the cops with this whole rape thing. It's really becoming a big deal. They need you to come down and tell your side of what happened after the costume party at In the Mix. Once you give a statement, they'll call Shannon back in for further questioning," I narrate.

Connor states, "I'll call the station today and arrange a time to give a statement. I see this is really outta hand. All of this over something that could've been handled in house, but it has spread like a wildfire. I only called you because we have unfinished business. This situation isn't settled."

I reply, "I know."

I give Connor the number to call the detective and he gives him a call. Connor reports to the police station the next day for questioning. He answers all of the questions they ask him and they end the interview. Now, since the cops have gotten our official statements, they call Shannon back to the interview room.

CHAPTER 13

Shannon is called back to the station for further questioning. She arrives at the station and the detectives tell her they have interviewed all parties involved, but they still can't bring charges on me. She's highly upset and doesn't understand why charges won't be filed.

"Ms. Bachman, I'm sorry, but your story is a bit outlandish and the other people involved aren't confirming your story," explains the detective. "It seems that you're the only one who has a story to tell that's different."

"Listen, I'm an attorney and I know the law. I won't stand for my rights being violated. I know what happened to me. If Connor didn't take my side, it's because he's mad at me. That's all," Shannon states.

"I understand you're upset ma'am, but you have to remain civil. We want to talk to you about this Connor fellow. We haven't caught up to anyone named Connor," says the detective.

Shannon is confused and states, "I thought you were going to call me once you interviewed everyone. You clearly talked to Connor already otherwise I wouldn't be here."

"Well, we've interviewed a guy who says he's your boyfriend named Mitchell Forestenhousler. He's on record stating that he's your boyfriend," reports the detective.

"You have got to be kidding me! This is a Mickey Mouse operation. I don't know anyone named Mitchell Forestenhousler. My boyfriend's name is Connor Bain. Damn idiots!" Shannon shouts.

"Do you have a picture of this so called Connor Bain? Why would all of the people you told us to contact not know him as such?" asks the detective.

Shannon responds, "I have no idea why they would say that. I don't even know if this incompetent department could even handle a stolen candy bar investigation. Yes, I have pictures of Connor."

Shannon shows the detective the picture and he confirms that the picture is of Mitchell Forestenhousler. The detective shows Shannon a picture of Mitchell's New Jersey driver's license. Shannon is totally befuddled. She demands that they call us all back in for questioning. She feels she needs to get to the bottom of this.

"Ma'am, we have some other stuff to talk to you about," says the detective.

"I won't talk about anything until you get them back in here. They're making me out to be some type of fool. They even have Emily in on it. I don't know what's going on," says Shannon. "I will lawyer up if I have to."

The detective doesn't want lawyers involved in this just yet, so he complies with her request to have us all come back for a group meeting. We're all willing to show back up for the meeting because we want this sorted out as soon as possible. This is a lingering conflict that needs to be resolved. I need my name to be cleared of all false charges against me.

Emily arrives at the station first. Moments later, I arrive. We wait for another thirty minutes for Mitchell to arrive. Shannon joins us in the conference room ten minutes later. The detective and another officer walk in behind Shannon.

"There's a lot of confusion and misunderstanding in this room today. We're here to get to the bottom of this situation today," states the detective.

They ask Emily and me what name we know Shannon's boyfriend by. We both answer with the name Mitchell. I tell the detective the same story I've told them already about how I've known Mitchell practically all of my life. Shannon calls us liars and states that we are in collusion against her. Mitchell also confirms his name again and that he has no idea as to why Shannon calls him Connor. Emily normally wouldn't be involved in helping me lie, but once I shared with her some damning evidence, she was all in.

"Officer, if you believe them, you're an asshole. I have no reason to lie. I'm successful, reputable, and beautiful. I gain nothing from making up wild accusations," Shannon states.

"Are you sure you can be trusted ma'am? Are you ready to discuss the other thing we need to talk to you about?" asks Detective Lewis.

"Yes, my name and word are golden. I would love to discuss this other thing that you keep mentioning. I'm eager to know what's so pressing," Shannon says.

The meeting with all of us ends. The cop tells us not to leave town because he may need to reach us for more questions. He keeps me and Shannon in the room with him and dismisses Emily and Mitchell. The detective tells Shannon that he's having a hard time buying her story because her integrity is compromised.

"I know you aren't basing your statement off of these lying fools. They have formed a cabal against me. Unfortunately for them, it's not going to work," Shannon reports.

"No, it's not solely from their statements. My opinion is based on common sense and this tape that Alex provided us with," says the detective.

"Tape? What tape? And what does common

175

sense have to do with this? Aren't you supposed to look at the facts?" asks Shannon.

"It's time to listen and stop talking ma'am. Your questions about the tape will be answered momentarily. I'll let you talk as soon as the audio file finishes playing," says the detective.

Before the cop turns on the recording, I think back to the first day Shannon came to In the Mix and asked me to work for her. I remember being upset and wanting to strangle her, but I didn't. How dare she solicit my help after sending me to jail and I was innocent? We sat in the booth and discussed what happened the night my life was changed forever.

I remember Sage set us up at booth three. I reluctantly agreed to work for Shannon that day because I needed the money. Before I left In the Mix that day, Sage gave me a bag filled with parting gifts. He gave me money, but more importantly, he gave me a recording from booth three. The entire conversation I had with Shannon was recorded with her admitting to falsely claiming I raped her.

I knew when the time was right, the recording would be beneficial to me and now is the time. The cop finally plays the recording and Shannon listens closely. Her facial expression turns from intrigue to horror as she realizes what the recording is revealing. I don't say a word, but I stare at her without blinking.

"I know what this looks like officer, but that's

old news and it has nothing to do with the current claim of rape. These are two totally different cases. Also, I didn't know I was being recorded and didn't agree to it, so that is inadmissible in court anyway," Shannon verbalizes.

I say, "Actually, the recording was made at In the Mix and it states on the door that the premises are under video and audio surveillance, so it's definitely admissible. Don't forget that you aren't the only one who knows the law. From what I recall, I was number one in our class. You were number two."

"Ms. Bachman, understand my position. You claim he raped you some time ago, but this tape seems to indicate that you lied about it. You say he raped you after a Halloween party, but Connor or Mitchell or whatever you call him says he is in fact the one you had sex with. Your credibility is very weak and there is no evidence to make us take Alex into custody. I have to let him go," explains Detective Lewis.

"This is an outright injustice. I can't believe you right now," Shannon says as she jumps out of her seat.

The officer tells Shannon that he may seek to prosecute her for filing a false police report and perjury. Shannon immediately states that she wants a lawyer. The interview ends and I leave. The detective allows Shannon to leave also because he hasn't filed any charges yet. Shannon storms out of the station, jumps into her car, and zooms away. I crack up laughing as she drives away. I've never seen someone so upset.

I leave the police department and head straight to Mullins and Philbert. I know Shannon's employer will be interested in hearing the recording Sage made for me. I'm very excited to let them listen to it. I go into the lobby of Mullins and Philbert to the receptionist's desk.

"How can I help you sir?" asks the receptionist.

I respond, "Hello, ma'am. I'm Alexander Huggins and I'm here to see Mr. Frederick Lester."

"I'm sorry Mr. Huggins. It must be an error on our part because I don't see your name down as having a meeting with Mr. Lester. I don't see it listed," she reports.

"No need to apologize because I don't have an appointment. I'm here because I really need to speak with the President Mr. Frederick Lester. It's a last minute thing," I vocalize.

"I understand Mr. Huggins, but Mr. Lester is an extremely busy man and really sticks to a stringent schedule. His schedule does not allow for walk-ins," states the receptionist.

I orate, "Ma'am I know he's very busy, but I know he'll make an exception for the urgent information I need to give to him."

"I'm sorry sir. I can't send you up, but feel free to make an appointment right now. He has some free time next week that I can pencil you in for," she remarks.

"No, it's okay. I'll just take my information elsewhere, but I hope your employer isn't going to be upset with you for costing the company another three million dollar block of business. Thank you for your time ma'am," I comment sarcastically.

The receptionist's face changes immediately when I mention the three million dollar block of business. I'm sure she wants to know how I know inside information about this company. Additionally, she doesn't want to be the person who's responsible for the company losing even more money. She immediately tells me to hold up for a minute.

She calls upstairs and speaks to someone in a position of authority. The person on the phone authorizes her to send me upstairs. I head for the elevator and go to the tenth floor. Mr. Lester's personal assistant, Carolyn, meets me at the elevator. His personal assistant is shocked to see me getting off the elevator.

"Alex, what are you doing here? Are you who the receptionist called me about?" asks Carolyn.

"Yes, it was me who she called about. I'm here because I have some information that may keep your company from losing more than the three million dollars it has already lost, but I'll only meet with Mr. Lester," I dictate.

"Alex, I'll be honest with you, he may not

want to meet you because the way things went south with you," Carolyn informs.

"I know he's upset about the way things went, but he'll see things differently after I present him with this information. Carolyn, trust me on this one," I verbalize.

"You can present me with the information and then I'll decide if he'll want the information himself. That should be fair," Carolyn offers.

I take her up on her offer. It makes sense for her to want to see what I have to offer. Also, I'm sure Mr. Lester doesn't want to see my face because of the rape I was falsely accused of committing. I was scheduled to start work here at Mullins and Philbert when I was incarcerated. Mr. Lester put his faith in me and was going to hire me for the position Shannon eventually got, but I let him down. He always spoke highly of me, so I'm sure he suffered some embarrassment stemming from my case.

Carolyn takes me into her office, so I can share my information with her. Carolyn listens to the recording from start to finish and her jaw is on the floor. She can't believe what she just heard. She is flabbergasted and immediately rushes into Mr. Lester's meeting. Mr. Lester ends his meeting abruptly and then Carolyn comes to get me from her office. Carolyn and I walk to Mr. Lester's office.

"Hello, Mr. Lester. Thank you for giving me a moment of your time. I know you're a busy man, but I wanted you to be privy to what I'm privy to," I say.

Mr. Lester says, "Young Alex Huggins, I never thought I'd see you in here again. I understand you have some important information for the company."

"Yes, I do sir. I too never saw me in here again," I comment.

I play the recording for him and he reacts the same way Carolyn did. He knows that this kind of information could ruin the company. Hearing Shannon incriminate herself about committing perjury doesn't sit well with him. Mr. Lester also knows that I could have taken this audio clip elsewhere and caused him a lot of harm.

"Alex, I always held you in high regard and that's why I wanted to hire you. I hope you know I had to keep the company's best interest at heart and that's why I distanced myself and the company from you. Also, I'm sorry you had to endure such pain and atrocities. We're grateful that you brought this information to us and didn't sell it to a news station. They would have paid handsomely for this information," Mr. Lester narrates.

Carolyn chimes in, "Not to mention our competitors would have paid a pretty penny too."

"Mr. Lester, I know you had to protect your clients. I totally understand that. That's why I came directly to you, instead of others. I never took what transpired between us personally," I pronounce.

"We owe you dearly. What can I do to repay you for this generous and unexpected largesse that you blessed us with?" asks Mr. Lester.

"Well, I'm very low on cash. I've been bartending to earn money, so I really could use a little hit to the pockets. Bartending in D.C. doesn't really pay the bills if you know what I mean," I recite.

"Carolyn will take care of that for you. That won't be an issue. I can't imagine that your place of residence is acceptable either if you're short on cash," says Mr. Lester.

"No, it's not sir. The neighborhood's not the best either," I reply.

"Put Alex up in one of our lofts. It's the least we can do for him. He's a friend of the company," says Mr. Lester.

"Thank you, sir. I really appreciate it. This means a lot. However, I want to be forward with you about the recording. The authorities are aware of its existence and may use it to prosecute Shannon," I state.

"Thanks for informing me and I totally understand. The recording will give you your life back. I'll use my influence to see that things go your way and for the company's sake try to keep this as quiet as possible," Mr. Lester replies.

"Maybe when this all blows over, I can be employed here as I was supposed to be before all of this happened. Please, keep me in mind," I shoot back.

Mr. Lester tells me that it's definitely possible once I'm fully vindicated of the charges I've been convicted of. Things are really looking up for me. I hope everything goes well for me. The meeting with Mr. Lester ends and Carolyn walks me out to get me set up with the items I've been promised.

"I'm not supposed to tell anyone this, but we are calling Shannon into the office later today. That's what Mr. Lester was meeting with those guys about when you arrived. We received an anonymous tip about her and started an investigation on her," Carolyn shares.

"I'm not surprised. She's dirty and I found out the hard way," I comment.

Carolyn gives me the things promised to me and I leave. Shannon's troubles are just beginning. Mr. Lester calls her into his office for a meeting. He has received information that she's the person who has dealings that caused them to lose the three million dollar block of business. Shannon is accused of money laundering and embezzlement. Her company and the authorities have opened up a full scale investigation into her financial dealings.

"What company did you use to run the background checks on the employees when you were assigned that duty?" asks Mr. Lester.

"I hired a friend of mine who's really good at that sort of thing," Shannon replies.

"Yes, I understand, but what company does this friend represent?" Mr. Lester asks.

"He's an independent contractor, but he has affiliation with Premier Investments. They're a very lucrative and reputable company," Shannon replies.

"You know Alexander Huggins right?" inquires Mr. Lester.

"Yes, I do. He was in law school with me and is the man who raped me," Shannon answers.

"I remember that case. I'm sorry that you endured such pain. It's unfortunate," states Mr. Lester.

"Thank you sir," Shannon replies.

The president asks, "Do you have any contact with him currently? Any affiliation whatsoever?"

"Yes, he's the independent contractor who helped me with the background checks. I know it seems crazy, but that's the truth," Shannon conveys.

Mr. Lester grills Shannon for an hour. He can't comprehend why she hired her supposed assaulter and a convicted felon to handle sensitive information. He questions her judgment and how she put the firm at risk of losing more than it has already.

"Sir, this will never happen again. I promise. I made a major mistake, but I will redeem myself. You know I'm good for it sir," expresses Shannon.

The president says, "Don't start with the

apologies now because there's more. Tell me what you know about Premier Investments and Mitchell Forestenhousler. You said that it's a profitable and reputable business, but only half of that is true. It is extremely lucrative."

Shannon declares, "The company invests in many things and has a diverse portfolio across the country. It's affiliated with many celebrities and sound organizations and I don't know Mitchell Forestenhousler. I know him as Connor Bain. We recently broke up, but he owns Premier Investments."

We ran a background check on Mitchell Forestenhousler and what we found may be startling to you. He owns Premier Investments, but uses it as a front for illegal drug selling and money laundering. He's been working with the District Attorney's office to help bring down other people who he's been working with. He's currently on trial for such activities and you hold close council with him. You can't fix this. We - the firm have no choice, but to sever all ties with you. You need to leave the premises immediately," Mr. Lester narrates.

"Sir, please. Don't do this to me," Shannon begs.

"You've done this to yourself. Too many poor judgment calls at the expense of the firm. Our clients deserve better from us," Mr. Lester conveys.

"I'll clean out my office sir. I understand,"

Shannon states.

"Your office has already been emptied. Security will escort you off the premises," says Mr. Lester as he motions security to enter.

Mr. Lester walks out while Shannon is crying and he doesn't look back. Two security guards escort Shannon off the premises and take her credentials. She's very sullen and dejected. She has no idea what started this shit storm she's in, but I do.

Before we went to Vegas, I dropped an anonymous tip to Shannon's employer letting them know that she's the employee who they were looking for in regards to being involved in some unethical proceedings. I let them know the reason they never got any results is because she was in charge of the investigation. Subsequently, they opened their own investigation while we were gone. The firm had no option other than to get rid of her. If their clients found out, the firm would have to close its doors. I also knew that the firm would turn over any information they have to the authorities to further protect themselves. The last thing any firm wants is a scandal.

Shannon calls my phone and I debate on whether I should answer her call or not. There's nothing she can do for me or to me at this point, so talking to her is pointless. On the other hand, I could get a laugh or two out of her. I decide to hit the ignore button and send her to voicemail.

If she calls back after that, then I'll answer it. A few seconds later, I receive an alert that I have a new voicemail message. As soon as I attempt to check the message, Shannon calls right back. I inadvertently answer the call.

"Alex, don't hang up. We need to talk and I really need to find Connor," Shannon states.

I reply, "I doubt we need to talk. Maybe you do, but I know I have nothing to say to you. Additionally, I don't know anyone named Connor, so stop saying that."

"Don't be this way Alex. We were tight at one point. Please. Everything's all fucked up and I have no other place to turn. If you won't talk to me, at least tell Connor… I mean Mitchell to give me a call. My entire world is falling apart," Shannon narrates.

"I'll let Mitchell know that you want to talk to him, but as far as I'm concerned our relationship is over. Please don't call my number ever again. I do have one thing to say before I hang up," I say.

"What's that?" Shannon asks.

I answer, "I'm glad you're able to experience how it feels to be riding high one moment and then have your life snatched from you in the blink of an eye. That's what you did to me! Life sucks bitch! That's some karma for your ass. I hope you enjoy it!"

I end the call without saying goodbye or anything, while she was in the middle of a statement.

CHAPTER 14

Two more days have passed with Shannon calling me about contacting Mitchell. Every time she calls, she always asks where Connor is. She knows I won't refer to him as Connor, but she still persists. Sometimes I think she's doing that on purpose to trip me up. For all I know, she may be recording our conversations to use as evidence that we fooled her into thinking Mitchell is some guy named Connor. However, I'm two steps ahead of her.

My last couple of days have been pretty relaxing. The police haven't bothered me about Shannon's bogus rape charge. They told me that it's a done deal for that case. I find pleasure in that. My new loft is not like the house Shannon rented for me, it's even better.

The best part about it is that it's free. The cops never bought her story about her rental home being for me. I never gave up my apartment and my parole officer vouched for me because he only visited me there. Getting Shannon to rent that house for me really helped to make her look guilty. Mitchell did me a solid when I asked him for his help. The conversation is still fresh in my head and I think about it all the time. We were at In the Mix throwing back a few beers when it all came together.

"Mitchell, I have another way to further incriminate Shannon. It'll be a classic way to really send her under," I uttered.

"Hey bud, if it helps you, you know that I'm all for it. Tell me what you're thinking. I know it's real devious," Mitchell replied.

I muttered, "It's real sick. I need you to beat me up bro. You know, rough me up a little bit," I said.

Mitchell stated, "Bro, I've wanted to beat you up ever since the seventh grade and I'll be glad to now since you asked me to, but I don't get how that will hurt Shannon."

As I laughed at his comment I replied, "Follow me dude. If you beat me up at my apartment, I'll make it look like I was attacked because I'm on the sex offender's registry."

"Oh, I get it. Shannon will feel like it's all her fault and want to help you get outta danger," Mitchell commented. "You have such a devious mind bro; I love it!"

"Bro, to go into law you have to be a schemer.

I may even spray paint rapist on the door or something to really sell her on it. Sage really put the plan together and I'll make it fit the law," I said.

"Sounds like a good idea, I have one even better. I'll write rapist on your back. I'm ready when you are," Mitchell remarked. "Once I heard the tape of her admitting that you didn't rape her, I wanted her to pay."

"Thanks a million guy! I will let you know when the time is right," I said. "Sage is even going to fake an attempt on my life at my apartment and at In the Mix. We have it all worked out."

Unfortunately for Shannon, her days are quite contrary to mine. Her days are filled with stress, worry and intense scrutiny. Ironically, her last few days are identical to the days when I was arrested and jailed for raping Shannon the night we celebrated passing the bar. I'd be lying if I said I feel sorry for her.

The D.C. police are at Shannon's house right now. They are bringing her up on charges for her wrongdoings. When they arrive at her house, she's totally shocked and in disbelief. She hurls many curse words at the police for coming to her home to arrest her. Nonetheless, her verbal assault and threats don't stop the cops from doing their job. She doesn't even know why she's being arrested.

"I'm an attorney damn it, I know my rights.

This charge is some total bullshit. You're picking me up and serving me with a search warrant for a perjury charge. This is really a waste of government resources and my time. You could be using your time to catch real criminals," Shannon explains.

"Ma'am, we're going to need you to step aside while we execute this search warrant. If not, we'll be forced to cuff you and put you in a patrol car. Ms. Bachman, we're not here for a perjury charge although we'll be addressing that too," Detective Lewis reports.

"Well, why the hell are you guys here then? What am I being charged with?" Shannon asks.

Detective Lewis states, "Ma'am, you're being charged with some very serious crimes. We're arresting you on charges of money laundering and embezzlement. You may want to call your attorney."

"You have to be kidding me. I've done no such thing. These charges are ludicrous. Money laundering and embezzlement, you can't be serious. My lawyer is really gonna eat your ass alive for this. I'm going to own this crappy department when this is all said and done," Shannon remarks.

The detective says, "We totally understand, but we need you to sit on that couch and let us collect our evidence."

Shannon promptly has a seat on the couch. She uses her time wisely and calls her lawyer. It's funny how she's an attorney and has to seek counsel for herself. As the cops look through her belongings, she tells her lawyer that he needs to get to her house now. Her lawyer arrives about twenty minutes later and looks over the search warrant.

He tells Shannon that the warrant is legit. The cops finish their search and remove several items from the house as evidence including her computers. The cops escort Shannon to their squad car and put her in the back of it. They even confiscate the Mercedes Benz that Mitchell got for her.

"You can't take my car too! I love that car. It was a gift. This is an outrage!" Shannon screams.

Shannon is now in the back of the squad car crying profusely. The gravity of the situation is now weighing down on her. She is about to be booked and charged. I know she never saw herself on this side of the law. I know I never saw myself there, never in a million years. The officer walks over to the patrol car and opens the door to speak to Shannon.

"Ms. Bachman, we have units at your other residence right now. We have a search warrant for that place too. Your attorney has been informed. I want to take this time to read you your rights," the officer explains.

Shannon replies, "I'm well aware of my rights and don't need you to read them to me. Also, dumb ass, I don't have another residence."

"Ms. Bachman, can you please refrain from using insults? Do you have a house that you are renting at 1210 Middlesex Street on the other side of town?" asks Detective Lewis.

"Oh, yes I do have a property that I'm renting at that address, but I don't reside there. I rented it for a friend, well at least I thought he was a friend," Shannon states.

"Right, I figured you would have something like that to say. Take her down to the station and we'll sort it all out down there," asserts Detective Lewis.

After a short ride, they arrive at the station. They escort Shannon to the interrogation room and begin questioning her in the presence of her lawyer. Shannon is still crying and pleading for this mess to go away.

Detective Brian Lewis says, "We have some serious charges that you're facing. Money laundering, embezzlement, tax evasion, as well as conspiracy to commit drug trafficking."

"My client is innocent of all of these charges. You guys know that my client is incapable of the things you charge her with. You must have gotten your badges out of cracker jack boxes," speaks Shannon's attorney.

Detective Lewis states, "We aren't so sure of her innocence. There are a lot of loose ends that need to be cleared up and also tons of evidence against your client. We want to hear her side of the story though."

"I'll answer his questions. The sooner I tell my side of the story, the sooner I can leave this hellhole," says Shannon.

"Tell us about the property you said you're renting for a friend. We need to know who this friend is and a good number to contact him or her on," replies detective Lewis.

Shannon replies, "The person is Alexander Huggins. He needed a safe place to stay, so I rented him the house. I never lived there."

"Is this the same Alexander Huggins who you say raped you some time ago and the same one you reported as raping you at the residence in question?" asks Detective Lewis in a sarcastic tone.

Shannon answers, "Yes, I know it sounds crazy, but that's the honest to God truth."

The entire room went silent at that point. Even Shannon's attorney is a bit confused. The million dollar question is: Why would you do anything for someone who raped you? The officer tells Shannon that he doesn't believe her story. He feels that she's telling an absurd story to save herself.

Shannon tells the detective that she felt bad for me, so she offered me a job and that all of this is stemming from that job. The detective gets a call and has to step out of the room for a moment. While he's out of the room, Shannon's lawyer talks to her about her involvement with me.

"This is not looking good. No one will believe

you befriended the man who raped you. To top it off, you're saying he raped you twice. Tell me what's going on here, so I can help you," says Shannon's attorney.

Detective Lewis returns to the interview room and states, "Our units at your other residence have interviewed your neighbors and they say they've never seen Alexander at your residence, but they described a man fitting Mitchell Forestenhousler's description there on numerous occasions with you. Tell us about that Ms. Bachman."

Shannon is frustrated. She informs the cops that this is one grand plot to frame her for something she didn't do. She tells them that she would meet Connor, well, Mitchell there from time to time, but that's it. Also, she says she would frequently meet me there to drop off work or my payments for work.

"The man, who hit you over the head and raped you in a parked car, is the same man who you employed, went to his place alone, and you rented a house for?" asks Detective Lewis.

"Exactly, that's what I'm saying," says Shannon.

Detective Lewis replies, "I know I can't be the only one who has a problem with your story. I'm sure your lawyer doesn't even believe this story. In fact, you don't believe your own bullshit story. We need the truth Ms. Bachman and we'll be ready for it when you offer it up."

Shannon sticks to her story, so the detective proceeds with his interrogation. He puts it all on the table to let Shannon know the severity of her dilemma and why it's crucial for her to come clean.

Detective Lewis states, "We have bank records showing that you wrote a check for fifty-thousand dollars from your account and that same check was deposited into the account of Premier Investments, which is a fraudulent company. We also have records showing money being withdrawn from the account of Premier Investments and that same amount of money being deposited into your account around the same time. We also have records of frequent withdrawals from your personal account for five thousand dollars being deposited into Premier Investments accounts, your rental property has drugs buried in the floor boards, as well as a Mercedes Benz registered in the name of Mitchell Forestenhousler who is a known drug trafficker and money launderer out of Linden, New Jersey and he's your boyfriend. The list goes on and on."

Shannon knows the law inside and out. She knows the evidence against her is rock solid. How could she not look guilty with all the ties back to her they have? Her lawyer wants to work out some sort of deal because he knows that Shannon can't win this case. Anybody with a tad bit of sense knows she's doomed.

"We need you to come clean about everything, otherwise we can't help you. You have to cut out this story about Connor and this Alexander rape case. Let's start at the beginning of all of this," says Detective Lewis.

"Okay, I really think they set me up. Alex and Connor or Mitchell. I'm so confused I don't even know the name of the guy I fell in love with. This is unbelievable!" Shannon comments as she cries.

"Why would they pick you out of all people to set up? Why would they waste their time sending or attempting to send you to jail? What's in it for them?" questions Detective Lewis.

Shannon puts her head down and states, "I think it may have something to do with the rape case that Alex was convicted and jailed for. I can't think of any other reason."

Detective Lewis asks, "So, that's really you on the audio clip saying that Alex really didn't rape you?"

Shannon reluctantly answers, "Yes, I was lying. Alex didn't rape me. He's obviously setting me up now for payback for me ruining his life."

"He's done a great job of getting you back if what you're saying is true. Alex's only connection to any of this is that he knows Mitchell from growing up in Linden with him. His financial situation is the same. He's clean. We need anything you may have to make us believe your story," says detective Lewis.

"That's just it. I don't have anything, but my word. I'm honestly telling you that I know nothing about any embezzlement or any other crimes. The only thing I did wrong was say my buddy Alex from law school sexually assaulted me when he really didn't. So, that's his motive for this entire concocted story," Shannon says.

"Go arrest him!"

"Ms. Bachman, you know the law better than that. We can't pick him up without having any evidence. If he's done what you say he has, then it'll come to light, but for now we are placing you under arrest. There's too much evidence against you and Mitchell confirms that you were well aware of all of his dealings. His deal has already been made with the courts. The facts show that you benefitted and profited from his illegal enterprise. Besides, you sent an innocent man to jail for nothing. That's deplorable. Book her," orders detective Lewis.

They take Shannon into custody immediately. She fights and resists, but her efforts are futile against the two officers. Her lawyer tells her not to worry and that he'll arrange bail as soon as possible. She's distraught because she's being charged with crimes she didn't commit. The cavity check that she's about to encounter will haunt her for the rest of her life, I'm certain.

The next day, I receive a call from detective Lewis. He informs me that Shannon confessed to falsely accusing me of rape and that he forwarded that information to the prosecutor of my rape case. He apologizes for the hurt I've suffered from Shannon's crime against me. He also states that the prosecutors are immediately filing a motion to have my charges expunged.

I won't be satisfied until it's done. I'm still a registered sex offender and as long as my name is on that list, I can't sleep well. Also, I still can't practice law, so until then, this good news isn't real. The day it becomes real is the day I'll be happy and celebrate. I thank him for his efforts to get my record cleaned up.

"One thing before you go Mr. Huggins," says Detective Lewis.

"I'm all ears," I utter.

"Ms. Bachman claims you and Mitchell set her up to take the fall for numerous criminal charges. Do you know anything about that? Do you have any insight as to why she blames you for her arrest?" Detective Lewis asks.

"Sir, I have no clue. I wish I could be of more help with your case. She was dating a friend of mine, so I saw her because of him. Outside of that, we had no interaction. I'm obviously a focal point of her rage. Maybe that's why she filed the false report against me to begin with," I say before we end the call.

CHAPTER 15

It's been six months since Shannon's arrest. She decided to fight her case and not accept the plea agreement she was offered. She has court today to find out her fate. The prosecution's case is so strong that Shannon can't win. I don't know why she didn't take the deal.

I guess she figures, since she's innocent of some of the crimes she's being accused of committing, that she'd fight to the bitter end. That's one hell of a gamble that she's taking. Mitchell testified against her in the money laundering case and his testimony was damning. He was even able to lessen his sentence for being a cooperating witness. I gave my testimony in court for Shannon's charge of perjury. My testimony was the same as it was the first time - the sex was consensual.

We're all sitting in court waiting to see what

the jury has decided. Moments later, the jury enters the courtroom and everyone is dead silent. All focus is on the jury. They're getting eye beamed by everyone in the room. Even the flies in the courtroom have stopped flying to hear the verdict.

"Has the jury reached a verdict?" asks the judge?

The jury's foreman responds, "Yes, the jury has reached a verdict."

The moment is very tense. People are on the edge of their seats. However, I'm not. I have nothing riding on this case, so it doesn't matter that much to me. I'm only here because I want to see Shannon's face when all of these guilty verdicts are handed down.

The clerk of court reads the verdict of guilty as charged. Shannon lets out a loud shriek over the courtroom. She screams out that her life is over. The courtroom gets very loud. The judge tells everyone quiet down and pounds his gavel. He demands order in the courtroom. The people promptly gain their composure. I'm satisfied with what I've heard and seen. Shannon's convicted and I see the look of hopelessness and despair on her face.

Court is adjourned and I walk into the hallway. The prosecutor who initially sent me to jail hands me a letter from the state. I open it up and read it eagerly. This is my letter stating that all my charges are expunged and I have no record of having a criminal record.

I log on to the sex offender registry to make sure I'm no longer on there. To my pleasant surprise, I'm no longer on the list. My dream has come true. The letter further states that I'm eligible to practice law with no preclusions or hindrances. I'm in a great spot because all of my patience and scheming has finally paid off. I was number one in my class for a reason. I'm fully competent, intellectual, and my doggedness is unrivaled.

I leave the courthouse and drive straight to In the Mix. I know Sage is there and I want to thank him for his help with the recording and letting me borrow his scheming mind. Without that tape, I'd still be a convicted felon. When I walk into the lounge, I'm all smiles. Sage knows only one thing could have me smiling so wide.

Sage says, "That smile could only mean one thing. In fact, the last time I saw you smile that big was when you were here celebrating passing the bar exam. Good for you man. Good for you!"

"I'm back! This paper certifies it. Thanks for the job you gave me when I needed it the most. You know the tape was priceless!!! That recording and working here gave me my life back," I say.

"Glad I could help, but I have to ask you something that I need clarification on," says Sage.

"Anything bro. Ask me anything," I say.

"Why didn't you take the recording to the cops when I initially gave it to you? Why wait so long?" Sage asks.

I answer, "That's easy. A perjury case would've been too easy for Shannon to beat. She probably wouldn't have lost her freedom or even gotten disbarred. I would have been practicing sooner if I would have come forward with the tape, but I knew that would come in time. I wanted her demise to be epic and newsworthy. The way I see it is that a fall from prestige hurts more than a fall from the unknown. Public embarrassment to the highest degree is what Shannon is dealing with right now. That was me not too long ago."

"I couldn't agree with you more. Very well played my friend. I've run some schemes before, but this is a classic. All parts of it came together perfectly. You're a very patient and meticulous person," Sage narrates. "I can't stop laughing at all of those threatening phone calls I made to you! The fake attempts on your life were some of my best acting!"

I say, "Thanks man. That's why I went into law in the first place. I'm pretty adept at seeing things even though I didn't see what Shannon did to me coming. I thought she was genuine. Your acting was very convincing!"

"Even the best of us get fooled sometimes," says Sage. "I may be the next Denzel."

"Tell me about it! I was hoping to thank

James too. He said he'd be here," I say. "I have to buy him a drink."

"If you're talking about attorney James, he's in the restroom. He went in there right before you walked in," Sage reports.

James walks out of the restroom and walks over to the bar where I'm talking to Sage. He's already heard the news from his sources that Shannon got convicted and that I have a clean record. I buy him a beer while we chat. I'm grateful for James' help with this situation.

I think back to the day when I initially asked James to get Shannon a job at the toughest firm in all of D.C. It's the firm I was set to work at before Shannon pulled her stunt on me. The requirements for their firm are very demanding. I knew it would only be a matter of time before she solicited my help. She was dependent on me in law school and I knew she'd try to further use me. I just had to be in position when she approached me. She always sucked at research and knew I excelled when it comes to research.

James was one of my best customers at In the Mix. He was a high powered attorney with a lot of influence. We were cool on a mentor/mentee relationship when I was in law school, but we became pretty good friends when I worked at the lounge. One day, I decided to ask him a favor.

"James, I know you have a great deal of influence at Mullins and Philbert. I need you to serve as a reference," I said.

He replied, "I know you are a cool guy and seemingly a good person, but with the felony rape conviction, I couldn't serve as a reference for you. I'd be putting myself in jeopardy and you wouldn't get the job anyway."

"I totally understand that. The reference isn't for me. It's for a friend. I know you have some clout at Mullins and Philbert, so maybe you could put in a good word for Shannon Bachman. She needs a job badly and was number two in our class," I narrated.

"What's in it for you?" James asked.

"I've known her since law school and have a vested interest in her having this job," I answered.

"Cool, I'm a firm believer in the notion of it's not what you know, it's who you know. If she checks out, consider it done," James stated.

"Thanks James, it means a lot," I said.

There was no better place or department to get her a job in. Nobody would be dumb enough to turn down a job at that company. It's too prestigious of a company to work for. Having them on your resume will catapult a person's career seemingly overnight. Contrarily, not accepting a job from them can send your law career into a premature grave. I put her in a no-win situation. She had to take the job with the only option of getting me to help her. Setting her up was simple after that.

I spend the rest of the day well into the night, celebrating my new life of being an attorney that's before me. This time it won't be so short lived. While I'm drinking shots and beers, a female approaches me. We hit it off from the first exchange of words. She wants to go home with me for a one night stand. Unfortunately for her, I know better. I'm either going home alone or I'll crash on Sage's couch in his office for the night and leave in the morning. I walk behind the bar to fix myself a final drink for the night. I don't think I've been behind this bar, since I stopped working here. This place gave me my life back.

It is so ironic how working as a bartender at In the Mix turned out to be extremely valuable. I remember when I first took the job here and I thought nothing good could come from this. I had feelings of inadequacy, but working here is what empowered me. I gained information that would change the course of my life forever.

Everybody knows that bartenders meet people from many walks of life. Bartenders serve teachers, lawyers, doctors, and the list goes on. It shouldn't be surprising because people from all walks of life enjoy adult beverages. I even gave some patrons of the lounge some great advice, but the knowledge I gained far surpassed any words of wisdom I dished out.

It was when I was working at In the Mix that I found out that my life was snatched from me on purpose. Cops are employed to serve and protect the public, but that's not always the case. I truly found that out the hard way. One night at the lounge, we barely had any customers because of a rainstorm. I wasn't even scheduled to work, but another employee called in sick, so I covered the shift. Boy, am I glad I covered that shift.

One customer who came in was a D.C. police officer. He was all stressed out over his partner being placed on administrative leave from the force. People are put on leave from jobs all the time, so I didn't think much of it. There was nothing going on in the lounge, so we had plenty of time to talk. I asked the cop why his partner was on leave. The direction the conversation went damn near knocked me off of my feet.

He told me that his partner was under investigation for being a dirty cop. I don't know much about a lot of things, but I do know that if his partner is a dirty cop then he is too. I didn't tell him that, but it was definitely on my mind. I allowed the conversation to keep flowing without conveying my opinion.

"What exactly do you mean by dirty?" I asked.

"Well, when I say dirty, I mean that he's accused of doing illegal things while being an officer," he said.

I must admit that I was intrigued to find out how dirty the cop was and what he was accused of doing. I had heard a million stories about dirty cops, but I didn't really think that they existed. On top of that, I've never knowingly been this close to one before.

"How many people did they say he killed? Did

he move kilos of drugs for a crime syndicate? It was something real juicy, wasn't it?" I eagerly asked.

He replied, "I can't speak about any of that type of stuff, but he's accused of taking bribes to look the other way on crimes he has seen."

I knew the cop shouldn't have been sharing any of that information with me because the investigation was active, but I didn't stop him. In fact, it seemed like the more alcohol he consumed the looser he became with his information. I was all ears. Strangely, I found the information interesting. The inebriated cop eventually told me about things he did that were unlawful without even realizing it.

I figured he was dirty too and was only in here that night to get inebriated because he knew it was only a matter of time before the investigation included him too. Let's face it; his partner is going to snitch on him as soon as he gets the first opportunity to cut a deal.

I said, "Hey bud, that's not too bad. All your partner did was close his eyes to a couple of things. That's harmless. Cops see people speeding all the time, but don't necessarily give the people tickets or even stop the people for that matter. I've even seen some things happen here that I could have or even should have spoken up about, but I didn't. That doesn't make me a bad person; it just makes me human."

"You're an alright guy. I guess we all have our

ways, but my partner has harmed a few people," he said as he gulped his beer.

"Oh no, Are you talking about murder?" I asked.

"You can't tell a soul. You have to promise," he spoke.

"Man, I don't have anyone to tell. Spill it," I said.

"There was this one guy who my partner harmed pretty badly. I mean fucked his whole life up. The crazy part is that he did it and never put a hand on the guy. He didn't even know him," he said.

I thought this drunken cop had one too many drinks because he wasn't even making any sense. He confused me when he stated that he harmed him, but didn't know him. I couldn't see how that was possible.

"What the hell are you talking about?" I questioned.

He told me about how his partner was approached by some hot young babe. She was giving him all the pussy he could ever have imagined. She was fucking him in the squad car, the movie theater, and wherever else she could get it. He didn't remember her name, but he knew she was a college student because she was always leaving books in the squad car.

Furthermore, he reported that the college girl said she had been raped by some guy she went to school with. He told me that his partner urged her to press charges, but she felt too much time had passed and that nobody would believe her anyway. I actually felt sorry for the woman because that's a tough spot to be in. There probably wouldn't be any evidence available to help her prove her story.

"What ended up happening?" I asked.

"The self-serving son of a bitch ended up going to jail for rape," he answered promptly.

"Justice prevailed then, but I'm interested to know how the prosecutor was able to get a conviction," I replied.

"Well, that depends on how you describe justice prevailed. The guy got convicted because the girl set him up. On the night she passed the bar exam, she faked like she got too drunk to drive home and got the guy she went to law school with to give her a ride home. This piece of shit is the same guy she said raped her in the past. During the ride home, she had sex with the guy," he explained.

My mind, at that point was seeing the direction that the cop's story was going in. I was instantaneously overcome with anger and rage. It was almost like I was being arrested again. I couldn't hold back my words.

"You gotta be fucking kidding me," I said.

The cop didn't know why I let that statement out. He thought it was because the story was so astonishing. He took it as a normal reaction to something so interesting.

He said, "Yeah, this is a true story. No bullshit. Let me finish the story."

"Go ahead," I responded.

"The girl… Shannon! That's her name. It just popped into my head. Shannon had the guy she was in law school with fuck her roughly in the car. You know, to make it seem like he raped her. My partner's role was to pull up on them in the car and act like somebody reported what looked like prostitution. Shannon played like she was nervous and afraid that she would lose her lawyer's credentials. Furthermore, she acted like he raped her right then at that moment. My partner took the guy into custody and he was charged," he narrated.

"That is one hell of a story! You can't make that stuff up. I am shocked," I said.

"Yeah, he didn't feel too bad at the time because he felt like he was helping to get a rapist off the streets. He knew it was wrong the way he went about it, but justice was served. Shannon's conniving ass even banged her head on the car to make it seem like the guy hit her over the head. Shortly after the case, the college girl stopped talking to my partner. Just went cold. It was almost like she used him for the case and wanted nothing else to do with him once it was done," he explained.

Of course this cop is talking about my case. Shannon told his partner a bogus story about me raping her to get him to help her out. I carried her through law school and all I got was a slap in the face. What a bitch!

From the moment I received that news, I was focused on paying her back. I know it hurts more to fall from a mountain top than it does to fall off a curb. For that reason, I launched a cabal that would take patience and planning. I wanted Shannon to experience a fall of epic proportions. I know jail will be harsh on her. She's so accustomed to the fairytale life she was living that she'll never adjust to the indecencies of prison. I'd be surprised if she doesn't kill herself the first night in jail.

EPILOGUE

I know what I've done to Shannon may seem cruel and excessive, but I beg to differ. I haven't done anything other than even the score. I'm a firm believer in an eye for an eye and a tooth for a tooth. Shannon ruined my life by thwarting my career before it blossomed and by having me locked away in a cage as if I was an animal. What she did never sat right with me. I abhorred seeing her and loathed working for her even more. I was fueled by rage from being raped. Not raped in the sense of being sexually violated, but raped in the sense that I was a victim of plunder. I was raped of having a successful career and bright future. She raped me of having a career where I would be a prominent member of society. The path I was on was blocked by Shannon's jealousy and selfishness. She couldn't handle being number two, but now she'll have to settle for a much longer prisoner identification number.